Phoenix Modern African Library

The Great Siege
of Fort Jesus

By the same author:

Dust and the Shadow

This is the epic story of the exodus of the people of Kush in search of Ophir, the Promised Land of Africa. We are taken across the vast continent in its primeval time; down threatening deserts, flooded rivers, the Great Rift Valley, forests inhabited by fierce wildlife and tribesmen, fire, thunder and pestilence.

In the process, Valerie Cuthbert weaves a compelling and touching story of tender love, stoic suffering and stately leadership. As in her first novel, *The Great Siege of Fort Jesus*, this novel is people by a crowd but each character is recognisable and, in many cases, lovable.

ISBN 9966 47 490 0

The Great Siege of Fort Jesus
An historical novel

Valerie Cuthbert

 PHOENIX PUBLISHERS, NAIROBI

First published in 1970
This edition published in 1988
by Phoenix Publishers Ltd.,
Grain Belt Industrial Park,
Sukari Industrial Estate,
Off Thika Rd., Behind Clay works,
P. O. Box 30474 - 00100,
Nairobi.

© Text: Valerie Cuthbert

ISBN 9966 47 093 X

Reprinted in 1990, 1992, 1995, 1999, 2002, 2006, 2011, 2021

Printed by
Autolitho Limited,
P. O. Box 73476-00200,
Nairobi, Kenya.

Acknowledgements

I have to acknowledge with thanks the following books for information on the history of Fort Jesus:-

"Fort Jesus and the Portuguese in East Africa" by C. R. Boxer and Carlos de Azevedo.

"Men and Monuments on the East African Coast" by James S. Kirkman.

My thanks are also due to my husband, Robert Cuthbert for his help and advice, and to Michael Livesey for reading and correcting my first MSS.

My characters are all either dead or fictitious. Although most of the names are genuine, their characteristics are from my own imagination.

Foreword

Fort Jesus is situated on a coral ridge that runs down to the mouth of the old harbour of Mombasa on what used to be known as the island of Mvita ("War"). It is situated in the Kenya Republic on the East Coast of Africa.

The history of Fort Jesus began when it was built on orders from Philip I of Portugal, who was Philip II of Spain. He had inherited the Kingdom of Portugal on the death of King Sebastian at the battle of Alcazer al Kebir in 1580.

The architect was an Italian Joao Batista Cairato. After working on the fortifications of Milan and Malta, he was sent to India where he was Chief Architect of India for thirteen years. Fort Jesus was his last assignment.

The Fort was built mainly by Mateus Mendes de Vasconcelos, during the period when Matias d'albuquerque was Viceroy of India, 1590 – 1597.

Since it was built the Fort has changed hands nine times: twice by trickery in 1631 and 1828; twice by assault in 1698 and 1746, when the defenders were insufficient to man the walls; twice by starvation in 1729 and 1828; once by bombardment with rockets and shell in 1875, and twice by negotiations in 1728 and 1837.

The Fort was taken over by the Imperial British East Africa Company and during most of the time East Africa (later Kenya Colony and Protectorate) was under British rule, it was used as a gaol. During recent years, however, it has been taken over by the Trustees of the National Parks of Kenya and is now a museum. For the first time in its long and turbulent history it is at peace and is open to the public.

MAIN CHARACTERS

Joseph de Britto	Aged 24 years. One of the senior captains of the Fort.
Maria da Costa	Aged 18 years. Cousin to the Prince of Faza, Prince Daud and Hussein.
Carlos Leao	Aged 9 years. Son of the Commandant.
Hussein of Faza	Aged 9 years. Friend of Carlos and brother of Prince of Faza and Prince Daud.
Rodrigues Leao	The Commandant of Fort Jesus when the story begins.
Hadija da Costa	Maria's mother and aunt to the Faza brothers (their father's sister).
Father Antonio	A much-loved Catholic priest.
Antonio Mogo de Mello	The Moor. Second in Command of the Fort. Later becomes Commandant.
Prince Mohammed of Faza	Prince of Faza Aged 17. Became Prince of Faza on death of father 1695.
Prince Daud of Faza	Aged 20 years. Cousin to Prince of Faza, Hussein and Maria da Costa.
Pedro da Sa	Unpopular officer infatuated with Maria.
Jose Barraso	A young Captain, later sent for help.
Luis Sampaio	Commander of the relief force.
Leonardo Nunes	Master Gunner of the Fort.
Jacome de Morais	A Portuguese officer who arrives at the Fort with relieving forces.
Sheikh Abdulla	A Muslim Priest and teacher to the Faza family.
Captain da Costa	Hadija's husband and Maria's father. Absent in Goa.

Chapter 1

The two boys had been fishing happily for about three hours and had caught quite a few brightly coloured fish of various sizes. Carlos Leao was just about to pull in another one when he happened to glance up towards the edge of a bluff which jutted out into the sea some distance away from where they were anchored.

He let his line go slack suddenly and his mouth fell open with surprise as he saw the sails of a big fleet of ships come into view. His freckles stood out as his face paled with shock and excitement.

"Look to the north, Hussein!" he shouted, his voice shrill as he shook his friend's shoulder.

Hussein turned, gasped and said: "What are they?" in an awed voice.

Both boys stared in fear and wonder as more ships sailed around the bluff until eventually there were seven great ships, quite unlike any others Carlos or Hussein had ever seen. There were also five smaller ships and around them sailed ten or eleven dhows.

The vessels moved slowly through the water for they were near the reef, and the breeze, which had been quite fresh earlier in the morning, had now died to a whisper. They had great sweeping sails, which, even as the boys watched, flapped lazily as they tried to catch the breeze. The boys could see a row of gun muzzles on each of the larger ships and knew, even at that distance, that they were not Portuguese ships. A big red flag, instead of the Portuguese emblem, flew on the masthead of the leading vessel.

Carlos and Hussein had heard discussions between the men in the Fort and knew that these cruel-looking ships could only be the fleet of the dreaded Omani from Muscat. They stared at them in fear, for they had heard of the cruelty and fierceness of the Arabs.

"They are the Omani come to attack Mombasa!" Carlos said at last with horror in his voice. "We must get back to the Fort at once and raise the alarm before our men are surprised."

Hastily pulling their fishing tackle and anchor into the bottom of the boat, the two boys paddled as quickly as they could back towards the Fort. The tide had turned and was with them and it aided them in their efforts to return quickly along the coast.

As Carlos paddled the sweat rolled off his bare brown shoulders, and as he felt the fierce heat of the sun he thought of how he had crept quietly out of his bed several hours earlier. There had been the coolness in the air that comes just before the dawn. In the east the sky was growing pale with the coming day, although to the west it was quite dark and one or two stars could still be seen. The pre-dawn breeze gently stirred the palm trees as the boy let himself softly out of his father's quarters in the Fort.

In the distance he could hear the Muezzin calling the faithful to prayer. Being a Catholic, he had already said his morning prayers, kneeling before the statue of the Holy Mother which stood on a small altar in a corner of his room; now he, was up and dressed ready to meet his friend, Hussein, who had promised to go fishing with him in the creek near the Fort.

The Fort towered over their lives, at once a guardian presence and a despot. A few days previously Carlos had seen his father and the Italian architect talking together.

Signor Cairato was the son of the original architect of the Fort. His thin greying hair stood on end as he ruffled it in agitation while talking to the Commandant of the Fort, Rodrigues Leao. He was attempting to get more building done on the Fort, but had come up against difficulties. It had already been under construction for many years, and the original plans had been changed so many times that the poor man despaired of ever seeing it completed.

The Commandant had spread his palms wide, shrugged his shoulders and, turning his eyes to heaven, had told the architect that he was asking the impossible. It was no fault of his that the labour was lazy and would not work.

"It's the damned climate," he sighed. "What can a man do? It saps all our health and strength!" He turned away, leaving Signor Cairato looking dejected.

The humid, damp, clammy climate, reduced a man to a limp wet rag, often making him shiver with the fever which rose from the swamps with the coming of night. Those mangrove swamps! And beyond them the war-like Musungulos who were always a danger to the garrison on the island. Some of them traded with the Portuguese and were, at a price, prepared to assist them, but others were allies of the Omani and were treacherous. Mombasa Island had only been in the possession of the Portuguese for a few years, and now, more than ever, they needed the great Fort to protect them from their many enemies.

Carlos and Hussein had been friends for many years, for Carlos had come to the island as a small baby with his parents; his mother had died three years before, and as the Commandant, his father, sought consolation in his work, so Carlos sought consolation in the friendship of Hussein, the young brother of the Prince of Faza. In spite of the difference in their religions, Hussein being a Muslim, they were like brothers, being the same age and more or less evenly matched in height, weight and temperament.

Carlos was short and sturdy with tow-coloured curly hair and blue eyes inherited from his gentle mother. Hussein, was also short and sturdy and had a mop of dark curls and soft brown eyes, a reflection of his mother who was one of the beauties of the Prince of Faza's harem. His father had been killed the year before whilst taking part in a punitive expedition against the Island of Pemba, under the direction of Carlos' father, who had been his friend. On his death his sons had moved into the Fort under the protection of the Commandant.

This expedition against Pemba had annoyed the Sultan of Muscat, and rumours brought in by spies all told of preparations being made in Oman for war against the Portuguese garrison of Fort Jesus.

However, on this morning of the 10th of March 1696, all had been peaceful, and war was far from the thoughts of the two nine year old boys who met in the courtyard of the Fort and were let out of the massive main gate by the sentry.

"Good-morning, young gentlemen!" said the man in a friendly manner as he opened the little door which was set into the great gate. "And where are you off to so early in the morning?"

"This is the best time to go fishing, Pedro," answered Carlos, who was usually the spokesman.

"You'll have a fine day for it, but it'll get very hot later on, mark my words! Bring me back some fish for my supper won't you?"

The boys laughed and scampered off, leaving him looking after them with a smile, and thinking of his own sons back in Portugal.

The buttresses of the Fort were still shrouded in greyness, but the golden fingers of the sun had started to touch the tops of the ramparts, bringing out the soft apricot-gold colouring of the stone and touching the mast where the flag of Portugal proudly fluttered in the breeze.

The sky paled to a light grey, which deepened into blue as the sun rose higher. It was still cool, but March is one of the hottest months on the east coast of Africa, just before the rains break, and the boys could feel the warning undercurrent of humidity as they made their way rapidly beyond the small settlement towards the creek.

They were both happy, and all their thoughts and talk was of the day's fishing. The creek stretched before them in the early morning light: the rays of the rising sun made the tops of the small waves dance and glitter. Even the leaves on the tall graceful palm trees shone and sparkled on this beautiful morning. There was a scent of freshly turned earth and vegetation around them, and Carlos drew deep breaths into his lungs with the sheer joy of living. It was a scent which would remind him of that day as long as he lived, for it was the last day of absolute freedom he was to know.

The boys walked down a small path to the edge of the water and there they found their boat, a small dugout canoe, hidden in the undergrowth where they had left it.

They launched it and pushed it into deeper water, then climbed in and paddled into the centre of the creek, where they threw out their anchor, and remained fishing for about half an hour without even a bite.

"There are no fish here today, Hussein," Carlos said impatiently at last. "We could stay here all day without a bite as the tide is still going out. I wish we could go outside the harbour and fish just inside the reef!"

"You know what your father told you!" cautioned his friend, but his eyes caught those of Carlos and held the same gleam of mischief.

They could look down over the side of the canoe into the shallow green water and see vast under-water forests of coral and marine plants swaying in the current. There were myriads of small, brightly coloured fish darting around, with now and then a glimpse of a larger shape moving lazily in the water. Fascinated by the beauty around them, engrossed in their fishing and talking, it had been some time before Carlos had glanced up and noticed the fleet of ships which now caused them so much alarm.

The boys paddled silently and steadily for some time but their arms grew tired. At last, rounding the corner into the harbour, they saw the Fort looming up strong and protective before them.

"Make straight for the steps, Hussein," gasped Carlos, and paddling swiftly they soon reached the gate at the foot of the Fort. They pulled their canoe up to the big stone steps, which were green and slippery with seaweed, and having tied it to a metal ring, they ran up to the Fort where Carlos immediately went in search of his father.

At last he saw him and rushed up to him shouting, "Father, Father! We've just come back from fishing along the north coast and we saw a big fleet of ships sailing towards Mombasa. They're still far off, but if the wind comes from the north they'll soon be here!"

"Calm yourself, my son, and tell me quietly why you disregarded my orders that you were not to fish outside the harbour? But perhaps we'd better deal with this disobedience later; now describe these ships to me!"

Carlos and Hussein eagerly described the ships they had seen and the Commandant looked very grave.

"Yes, it sounds as though these are Omani ships, so thank God you've been able to warn us, for now we'll be able to prepare ourselves for battle."

Rodrigues Leao wasted no more time and at once sent men out in a boat to confirm what the boys had told him. When they reported back that they had seen the fleet of ships lying out to sea becalmed, the Commandant had the big gun of the Fort fired as a warning to the men on the island that they were under attack and were to report immediately to the Fort. He knew that there were no ships expected from Portugal or Goa and these could, therefore, only be hostile battleships from Muscat.

He called an emergency meeting of all his officers and ordered that the Fort must immediately be provisioned for a long siege, and arrangements must be made for supplies to continue from the outside in case of emergency. He then sent his officers running off in all directions to execute his orders.

Carlos and Hussein watched all these preparations with great excitement as it was the first time they had seen the Fort being made ready for war.

Nothing more was said about their going out of the harbour without permission and Carlos knew his father was far too busy to mention it now. He was glad they had disobeyed orders this time, for it had enabled them to give good warning of the threatened danger.

Chapter 2

All night the drums had been beating – thrump thrump thrump, thrump thrump thrump – on and on, deep, mysterious and strangely fear-inspiring. All night long Joseph de Britto had tossed and turned in the heat of the March night: wet with sweat his naked body longed for the relief of a breeze, but it was the hottest month of the year and almost impossible to find coolness anywhere and certainly not in the small room where he lay in the officer's quarters of Fort Jesus.

He had a dull headache, caused by the heat, sleeplessness and the incessant beating of the drums, the sound of which seemed to echo and re-echo through his tired brain. He shivered, but not with fear, for he was a brave man, but with the feeling that there were mysterious goings-on in the blackness of the night outside.

He knew that there were hostile Africans on the mainland where the drums were sounding and that armed Musungulos made very short work of any man unfortunate enough to fall into their clutches. Although at this particular time most of them were outwardly friends of the Portuguese, this friendship would only last for as long as the Portuguese were strong and willing to trade with them. Having attempted to attack the Fort on a few occasions, only to be beaten back with heavy losses, they now seemed to realise that it was well defended and so they made an outward show of friendship. But they still watched for any signs of weakness and many of them would be only too willing to assist the Omanis (or help destroy them) should the opportunity arise.

Joseph went on to think about the ships which had been sighted three days previously. There had been a dead calm prevailing since then and it was not possible for ships to approach near the harbour unless a strong north wind blew. The fleet came and went on the horizon and had been doing so since the first day it had been sighted.

The enemy had lost the advantage of surprise which was so essential for success and the defenders were ready and waiting for them. Most of the preparations had been completed for a siege and, on this Day of Grace, the 13th of March 1696, there was a strong force of armed men in the Fort, composed of just over 50 Portuguese: there were also 2,500 Swahilis, including women and children.

The courtyard was piled high with food and carcasses, and men were busy storing all the provisions which had been hastily brought into the Fort and dumped down haphazardly during the past two days. There were herds of cattle, sheep and goats and baskets of protesting chickens; huge sacks of grain and beans; dried meat, kegs of salted meat; barrels of flour and oil; and piles of coconuts ready husked.

Mercifully there was plenty of sweet, fresh water, for not only were there two deep wells in the courtyard inside the Fort, but also another one in the dry moat under the walls where many people had taken refuge.

The Fort was crowded to capacity, for many people from the town had sought refuge, and there was a jostling, colourful, noisy throng of people moving in and out of the crowded courtyards.

The poorer people took refuge in the dry moats around the castle, where the overhanging walls and banks gave them some protection from the weather. Joseph had watched the arrival of several of the wealthy merchants of the town with their families and slaves. These men strutted along, full of self-importance and arrogance. They were richly dressed in silk robes worn over their full, ankle-length pantaloons. Great frills frothed out round their necks and on their heads they wore large, soft, flat hats which were ornamented with jewels.

Their women, who proudly followed behind them, wore long flimsy veils over their dark hair, to which they had fastened jasmine or frangipani flowers, which gave off a sweet perfume as they passed. They were richly dressed, and wore very full skirts over many petticoats, and had silk scarves of many colours crossed over their breasts. They were accompanied by tall slaves, who held umbrellas to protect them from the fierce sun. These slaves were dressed in jerkins and wore knee-length pantaloons and turbans.

"Make way! Make way!" the slaves would shout as they forced a path for their masters and mistresses through crowds.

Joseph stood by the gate of the Fort and watched them pass. He also saw a crowd of women from the town; some of them were the wives and daughters of the Swahili soldiers. These women wore gaily coloured *kikois*, covered with a black *buibui*, which they drew shyly over their faces when in the presence of men, revealing only their dark eyes. They all wore sandals on their narrow feet, and were, for the most part, quiet and shy.

It was amazing, reflected Joseph, how all these people had somehow fitted in and around the Fort. The soldiers slept in odd corners amongst all this confusion of movement.

Normally many of them slept in houses in the town, which were situated in the dark, narrow cobbled streets. These houses were built with overhanging wooden balconies, and had beautifully carved wooden doors. But since the enemy ships had been sighted, the Commandant had issued an order that his fighting force must be concentrated in the Fort. So the men were all billeted in Fort Jesus with the exception of a small garrison at Fort Joseph, which had orders to fall back on the Fort in an emergency.

There were groups of men working feverishly on the many tasks needed to make the Fort ready for war. The guns, which were all cleaned and primed, at last stood ready for instant action, their piles of cannon balls stacked beside them and fires constantly kept alight beside them. Some of the weary gunners lay asleep next to their guns.

The defenders had been given three days grace in which to prepare and had made the most of their time. By superhuman efforts they had performed miracles and were now ready to face whatever menace the Omani fleet held.

Joseph eventually gave up the attempt to sleep and decided to dress and go out on the ramparts where he hoped it might be cooler. Rising from his hot bed, he washed himself at the basin in the corner of the room by the light of a candle. This done, he put his legs into the pantaloons which reached down to his ankles and then drew on his boots. Next came a long-sleeved shirt over which he put a thick leather jerkin; then he adjusted a clean white linen frill around his neck to his satisfaction, and finally buckled on his sword.

He glanced at his steel armour, but left it hanging on its hook on the wall. He would put it on later. It was too hot to wear it just yet. He also left his cloak, which normally swung from his shoulders, but put on his cone-shaped, pleated black hat as he opened the door of his little room and made his way out. Being a senior officer, he had a tiny room to himself – the junior officers, however, had to share their quarters!

Chapter 3

It was bright moonlight outside and Joseph walked up and down the rampart passing the sentries on their beats; they were all very much on the alert for the slightest sign or sound of danger. He noticed they too were dressed for war, with breastplates gleaming in the moonlight over their usual leather jerkins.

Apart from the throbbing drums, which sounded louder now he was out in the open, there were the many noises of the African night. Distant cries and sounds rose from the moat and the town far below them; a dog barked in the distance; insects chirped and squeaked; birds called, and suddenly there was a faint rustle from the palm trees as a slight breeze sprang up and the leaves whispered and swayed like dancers.

The breeze was welcome in relieving the sweltering heat; but it also brought a threat: for it came from the north and even as he looked out to sea through his spy-glass, Joseph thought he could see the white sails of the enemy fleet gleaming in the bright moonlight in the distance. He knew that in another three hours, or less with a good breeze, the enemy would be approaching the entrance of the harbour.

He stood there for a few moments longer, but although the moonlight was conducive to dreaming, he knew that once the Fort was roused he would have many tasks to keep him busy. He must first attend the early morning Mass, after which it would be a case of waiting for action – and the unknown.

His thoughts turned briefly to Maria da Costa. "She must be sleeping now," he smiled at the thought, but his eyes were still searching out to sea.

Maria was beautiful – in fact the most beautiful woman he had ever seen. She was only just out of her girlhood, and had a sweet but proud face with high cheekbones and perfectly shaped nose and mouth. She was tall and slim, but her figure was that of a woman. Her long brown hair gleamed as it rippled in waves over her shoulders, and her blue eyes fringed with dark lashes, gleamed with sudden flashes of merriment. She had inherited her blue eyes and her laughter from her father, Captain da Costa. He had once wooed and won the heart of Hadija, the sister of the Prince of Faza, who had defied her family to marry him on condition she was allowed to keep her Muslim faith.

However, Maria was not sleeping as Joseph thought. She had been lying awake quietly for some time, one arm behind her head. A beam of moonlight through a gap in the window shutter had awakened her, and the heat prevented her from going back to sleep.

She now lay thinking of the tall, slim young man with the physique of an athlete, who had looked at her so often during the past few weeks.

He had recently arrived from Goa and Maria had noticed him glancing at her with sudden awareness in his eyes. She had not seen him before and asked her cousin, Prince Daud, who the new Captain was.

"That's Captain Joseph de Britto," her cousin said with a smile. "He has come out to take the place of your father while he's away, so he's now third in importance after the Commandant. In spite of his youth, he has the reputation of being an expert swordsman as well as a brave soldier. His family is old and respected and owns vast estates in Goa and Portugal. One day he will inherit them."

"Is he married?" asked Maria with a slight blush.

"No, my fair cousin, and I've heard that he prefers soldiering to women, although all the mothers in Lisbon and Goa tried to catch him for their daughters – he is still fancy free and no doubt intends remaining that way. Come with me, Maria, and I'll introduce you to the gallant Captain!"

Maria walked with her cousin to where the Captain stood alone looking out to sea over the ramparts.

Maria could picture him as he had stood then, with his smooth olive complexion and black hair; his long face had a rather melancholy expression, until he showed his splendid teeth in a sudden heart-warming smile. He had turned towards them as they approached him. Maria then saw he had warm, brown eyes and long slim hands. She heard him speaking to her cousin and liked his deep resonant voice. He bowed low as they were introduced, and Maria had felt herself blush under his frank, admiring gaze.

She lay in bed now, remembering that introduction, and realised with a pang that, although this young man was a stranger to her, she was terribly afraid and anxious for his safety in the coming battle.

The soft light of the dawn was beginning to streak the sky as she heard the call of the Muezzin in the town below them. Her mother had risen earlier and was quietly reading the Koran by the light of a small lamp. Maria rose softly and began to dress.

Her mother heard the slight sound and when she saw Maria getting up she looked towards her and smiled. After greeting her she said, "I see you too are going to pray, Maria! It is a good thing to pray when danger threatens. Although we belong to different faiths, we pray to the same God for protection and victory over our enemies."

"I do wish Father were here, Mother!" Maria said with a little sigh, as she slipped a pale grey silk gown over her head. "It's a shame you had to stay here without him."

"Yes, I miss him very much and wish he were here, but he knew it would take many weary months and a lot of tiresome travelling before he could settle his father's estates in Goa. He may even have to go to Portugal before he returns, so he thought only of my comfort and safety when he left me behind. He never dreamt of an attack on the Fort in his absence! We can only pray for his safety and wish him speedy return."

"I'm sure he knows how often we think of him, and will be impatient to return," said Maria softly, as she finally finished her preparations by flinging a white lace veil over her dark hair. Then taking her rosary and prayer book, she smiled at her mother as she left the room they shared in her father's absence, and descended to the Chapel where men and their women were gathering.

A slight movement next to her startled her for a moment, and she turned quickly to see she had been joined by Joseph de Britto.

"Why! I thought you would still be asleep," he said after greeting her with a bow.

"No – It's very important that I go to Mass today," she said softly.

"Please pray for me too, Maria," he said, using her name for the first time. His voice was deep and soft.

She glanced at him, startled, and seeing the warmth in his eyes, looked down in sudden confusion.

"I'll pray for you with all my heart," she said shyly.

She entered the coolness of the Chapel, crossed herself, genuflected and sank to her knees in prayer in the pew reserved for the officers and members of their families. Joseph followed suit and the two young people remained thus, while other members of the congregation joined them to pray for help and strength on this momentous day.

Chapter 4

Father Antonio was very uncomfortable. He was fat, and the hot weather, coupled with the fact that he wore a robe of thick brown wool, made his life a purgatory. He was covered with prickly heat which burned and itched unceasingly and he had scratched himself almost raw without relieving the terrible itching. He found it very difficult to endure his suffering with patience, and was quite sure his troubles had been sent by the Devil to torment him for indulging himself with good food, wine and a soft bed. The onset of the hot season had been the start of his torture and, as a consequence, he found it very difficult to maintain his usually happy disposition.

His stomach and double chin quivered as he heaved a great sigh, and rolled heavily off the bed to start the new day. He washed himself in the tepid water standing in an earthenware bowl in the corner of his room and put on his heavy robe and sandals and made an effort to tidy his bushy hair and beard. Then with another sigh, he went off in the direction of the Chapel.

It was dawn, and the birds were waking up and calling to each other in the trees outside the Fort. He made his way into the dark Chapel, where he knelt at prayer for some time before the statue of St. Anthony. He rose feeling calmer and more at peace with the world.

He busied himself with preparations for the Mass he was soon to celebrate, and shortly the Chapel was a blaze of light as he went round kindling the candles on the altars.

He knew from the increased wind that today would probably see the commencement of the expected attack, for the ships which had been becalmed could now fill their sails and ride into the harbour. He knew too, that as battle was imminent, he would hear many confessions.

"It's strange," he thought, "how men always turn to God in times of danger or trouble, and forget Him again when things are going well with them!"

He was ready for the Mass now, and going outside, signalled to one of the boys who was waiting to start ringing the bell. The Chapel filled and soon the rows were filled with men, with a few women and children scattered amongst them.

The Priest saw the bowed heads before him and prayed silently and sincerely: "Protect them, O Lord, in their danger, and comfort those who love them."

He moved towards the altar and as the service began, the congregation forgot he was a fat old Priest who suffered from the heat like themselves. At that moment of truth he became endued with the dignity of God's representative. It was a solemn moment, with danger winging its way fast towards them, and the Priest and congregation joined together to pray for deliverance from their enemies.

As the Priest's voice rose in a Latin chant, the thoughts of his congregation were many and varied.

The Commandant's thoughts were not entirely holy, for he had the welfare and responsibility of thousands of people on his shoulders. He was wondering whether he had forgotten to take some precaution which might mean life or death in the battle ahead.

His son, Carlos, was acting as acolyte and was automatically swinging the censer with the fragrant incense, but at the same time his thoughts were of his mother. He would have liked to have run to her to tell her about sighting the ships, for he felt she would have been proud of him. Sometimes he remembered the touch of her hand on his head; softly smoothing back the hair from his forehead; he could remember the fragrance of her perfume, and her soft blue eyes and golden hair. He had been six years old when she had died from fever, and he still woke up at night when he had been dreaming and called out for her, until he remembered she had gone forever. He was, after all, still a very little boy at heart who sadly missed his mother.

Joseph de Britto and Maria were very conscious of each other, and in spite of the solemnity of the occasion, their minds were not on the service. There was a sharp awareness of each other which they could both feel, although they neither looked at each other nor spoke, and outwardly appeared to be concentrating on their devotions.

Pedro da Sa's head was reverently bowed on his hands and to an observer it would appear as though he were praying, but his thoughts were far from prayer. He profaned the holiness of the Chapel, for they were concentrated on the lovely Maria whom he could just see through his finger. He had seen her enter with Joseph de Britto and now his evil mind seethed with jealousy.

Pedro was disliked by both officers and men, for he was harsh and overbearing to those under him, and obsequious to those he considered his superiors. His full red lips, heavy eyelids and fleshy hands showed him to be a sensualist, and he never lost an opportunity of boasting about his conquests. He had the idea that he had only to smile at a woman in a certain languid way, for her to be prepared to give herself to him, and it hurt his pride when Maria was aloof towards him, yet friendly towards Joseph. Like Father Antonio, Pedro da Sa was having restless, disturbed nights, but it was not heat that obsessed him, but thoughts of Maria.

Antonio Mogo de Mello was well aware of his position and responsibility as Second in Command of the Fort. He knew that his nickname amongst his men was "The Moor", and he admitted that it suited him well. He was very tall, with a dark tanned skin and full black beard; he walked with a slight limp, as the result of a wound received in battle in his youth, but he was a tough, old warrior.

He concentrated whole-heartedly on his prayers and on receiving the Sacrament, for he was a brave, sensible man and a good Catholic. He knew that no worry on his part could alter future events for better or worse. Whatever God had ordained would happen – was his Eastern kind of philosophy.

He would have liked to have been a priest, for his natural inclination was to devote his life to prayer and study, and he had in his youth contemplated entering a monastery. But his father, Luis de Mello, had sailed as a Captain with the great Vasco da Gama, and it was his one wish that his only son would become a soldier like himself. So, after a brief argument, Antonio had given in and followed his father's wishes. He had lived a hard life but a very full one, and on the whole did not regret his decision. He lived an austere and celibate life and was shy in the company of women, although many women had looked at his dark good looks – like a black eagle. He had never loved and never considered marriage, not even to carry on the family name.

Next to him Jose Barraso knelt in prayer. He prayed earnestly for courage, for he was the youngest officer in the garrison and this would be his baptism under fire. He was very young and slightly-built, and the hair on his chin was still soft and light brown. He was very proud of his beard, but it hardly merited that name yet, and somehow it made him look even younger than he was. Like a lot of small men, he was inclined to assume a pompous air of self-importance in order to hide his feeling of insecurity, and he was quick to draw his sword at imagined insults.

The older men treated him with an amused tolerance which made him furious but, as he was the most junior amongst them, he dared not take offence. However, he recovered his self-esteem by being a strict disciplinarian with the men under his command. He had been put in charge of the guns at the Fort, having been posted to Mombasa from Goa. He had just completed his military training in Portugal, which had included a course as a gunnery officer.

His men were inclined to be amused by him, but made a great show of obedience and listened respectfully when he gave them long lectures on armaments and artillery. Most of them were old enough to be his father and had seen much hard action in their lives.

The one man in his command who made no secret of his contempt for him was his Master Gunner, Leonardo Nunes, whose surly taciturn disposition made him unpopular with the other gunners, although he was first-class at his job. There were rumours he had been forced to leave Portugal for killing a man belonging to an important family; but he never spoke about himself, and his nature and appearance did not encourage friendship, and no one enquired too closely into his past.

His face was wrinkled and tanned like a piece of old leather and he carried the pockmarks of an old attack of smallpox, as well as one or two scars from knife-wounds. His body was short and thick set, like that of a wrestler, and his shortcropped hair was grizzled grey.

It was known that he lived with a Swahili woman, by the name of Fatima, outside the Fort, and had a small son by her. This child, who was now about two years of age, was the apple of his eye and the only soft spot in his hard heart. Rumour had it that he had turned Muslim, but the look in his small brownish-green eyes forbade any questions and now he too was in the Chapel, kneeling and praying with the rest of the men.

Mass came to an end and they all left the Chapel, each with his secret thoughts, hopes and fears.

As the congregation filed out, Father Antonio called back four of the men saying, "My sons, we are all in great danger this day and my prayers have been to our beloved Saint Anthony. I have had guidance and know that he wishes to watch closely over us and guard us during our time of peril, therefore come with me."

The old priest led the puzzled men to the statue of the Saint which stood above an altar at the side of the chapel. He looked up at the figure which stood above them with its right hand raised in blessing.

"Take him down, my children, and dress him in soldiers' uniform," said the old priest.

The men silently and reverently obeyed, and when the statue of the Saint was dressed to the Priest's satisfaction, they lifted it onto their shoulders, and with Father Antonio leading the way, carried it to the walls of the Fort. Under his directions, they placed it in a prominent position, where it would be visible from the sea, as well as to the defenders of the Fort. The four men then knelt while the Priest blessed them.

Chapter 5

Maria and her mother lived in the Fort in Captain da Costa's quarters. The Captain had received news that his father was dying and had hurriedly left on the last ship which had sailed from Mombasa to Goa. He had left his wife and daughter in the care of his wife's nephew, Mohamed, Prince of Faza, and his cousin Prince Daud. It was not known how long he would be away, for it often took many months to journey to Goa to settle estates. His father had estates in Portugal as well, which could easily mean an even longer absence.

The Prince of Faza was only seventeen-years of age but had already proved himself to be a brave soldier during the punitive expedition to Pemba the previous year, when his father had been killed. The youth had taken command and had avenged his father's death.

He was full of life and joy; with his flashing black eyes, dark curly hair and stocky build. He was beloved by all who knew him, and Sheikh Abdulla, the old man who had been his teacher and adviser since the death of his father, loved him like a son and handled him as he would a high-spirited horse. Hussein (Carlos' friend) was his brother, and it was obvious that when he grew older, he would be exactly like him.

Prince Daud was his cousin, but there was such a marked contrast between them that people wondered how they could be blood relations at all. Prince Daud was older, being 20 years of age; tall and slim with the aquiline features of an ascetic and a poet. He had a neatly trimmed black beard and spent most of his time in study and contemplation. However, although Prince Daud was gentle and a philosopher, he was brave like the rest of his family, and reared on great traditions. He was like a finely tempered steel blade which had yet to be tried. He had not been with the expedition on which his uncle had been killed the previous year, so had never been proved in battle. He had, however, a hidden fire and strength which would stand him in good stead when his time of testing came.

Maria's mother and the other women were busy organising a place where the wounded could be cared for in safety.

Hadija's hair had a few streaks of grey and she had a sad expression, for she missed her gay husband. However, she was brave and capable woman and now bustled about with great energy supervising the preparations for a hospital.

A large storeroom was cleared out and there Hadija had put mattresses filled with freshly cut grass in rows on the floor. The doctor had died suddenly a few weeks ago and so far no replacement had been sent to the Fort. However, most of the soldiers were used to treating the wounds of their comrades on the battlefields, and all the women were used to nursing seek and wounded men.

Hadija, like most of the women of her time was considerably skilled at nursing, and she even kept the doctor's instruments ready in case they were needed. Bowls and basins were put ready, as well as containers full of water, or wine. There was also a precious supply of opium, which had come from China via Goa, where it was known to be a painkiller. Small stoves were set up in one corner for boiling water and cooking food, and a supply of bandages, splints and soothing balms were kept ready.

Methods of treating patients were, of necessity, crude but, mused with care and devotion and the wounds kept clean, it was amazing how men often survived the most terrible injuries and illness.

Maria was helping her mother to prepare for the wounded. She had great sympathy and compassion and her mother had trained her well in the art of nursing; so she had no fear of fainting or being sick at the sight and smell of blood.

"Hurry up, Maria!" her mother said. "We have to work swiftly, for now that the breeze has risen the Omani may be upon us before we're ready."

Maria dashed about, her clothes clinging to her slim body, for she was soaked through with perspiration. The walls of the Fort were thick and no breeze penetrated to the place where the women were working.

The sun had risen high above the horizon by this time, and there was a lot of noise and bustle as men and women went about distributing rations under the personal supervision of Joseph de Britto. The Commandant had ordered that everyone be fed immediately after Mass, for men fought better on full stomachs.

They had hardly finished their meal when the alarm sounded and voices shouted throughout the Fort the stirring cry of "To arms! To arms!"

They could hear the sound of drums and chanting coming nearer from the direction of the entrance to the harbour and there was a rush to take up their defensive positions.

The waiting was over. The enemy had arrived!

Chapter 6

From the vantage point of a lookout tower built on the corner of the bastion of St. Mateus, which commanded a view of the harbour mouth, Joseph de Britto shaded his eyes from the sun and saw seven great ships under full sail entering the harbour, followed by five smaller vessels and several dhows.

As they approached the Fort he could see that each one was full of shouting, yelling men. They were armed to the teeth with swords, daggers and shields; some of the men were beating away at big drums, clashing cymbals and blowing large horns. The ships sailed into the harbour and swept towards the Fort one after the other like birds of prey, confident that victory would be easy, as they could see no movement from the Fort.

Joseph noticed that the seven big ships had three masts and were similar to the Portuguese war ships, having high, beautifully carved sterns like little castles. He recognised the vessels from the descriptions he had heard. Yes! these were the Sea Hawks, the famous galleys of the Omani Commander, Big Ali. He was famed throughout the Arab and Christian world and feared on the coasts of Africa and the eastern seas for preying on the shipping which sailed to and from India and China. His misdeeds and cruelty were notorious!

The Commandant of the Fort had been biding his time and waiting for the enemy to get as close as possible before he at last gave the order: "Fire!" The silence of the Fort was shattered as with a great noise and clouds of smoke the big cannons simultaneously opened fire on the intruders. The surprise was complete and the fleet fell into confusion as the defenders in the Fort saw splashes falling all around the ships.

The mast of one of the ships fell with a crash and a tangle of rigging, as it was shattered by a cannon ball. The ship slowed down, out of control, and as it did so, the current seized it and drew it rapidly towards the reef. Its crew could be seen running around like disturbed ants and the watchers saw the ship drifting towards the reef which was just out of sight.

Carlos and Hussein were wild with excitement! Although they had been told to keep safely out of the way, they had found a vantage point from which they could see the whole battle.

"A hit! A hit!" shouted Hussein when the mast of the ship shattered and fell.

They rushed over to the other side of the Fort to find out if they could see where the ship had drifted, but to their disappointment it had been thrown onto the reef just out of their view.

There was a shout of "They're moving off." Yelling, "Come on, Hussein!" the two excited boys once more raced across the Fort to their first vantage point, followed by a curse or two as they got in the way of a sweating gunner.

The Omani ships had, indeed, turned away from the battle, firing a few shots in the direction of the Fort as they went. Joseph could hear quite clearly the orders that were shouted from ship to ship as the remaining vessels withdrew to the other side of the harbour entrance. They then sailed down the harbour towards the creek, carefully keeping out of gun-shot on the other side of the channel, and making no move to attack the Fort. The first round of the battle had definitely gone to the defenders!

The smoking guns fell silent as the enemy withdrew out of range and Jose Barraso was seen running around giving orders to everyone. The gunners were busy swabbing out the guns and getting everything ready for the next attack, which they all knew must come fairly soon. The enemy, surprised at the fierce opposition and the sudden firing, as well as by losing a ship, had withdrawn out of sight to take stock of the position. So far the initiative had been with the defenders, but next time they might not be so lucky.

There was a lull for about an hour, then a messenger came running to the Fort, shouting that the enemy had landed down the creek and were off-loading supplies and at least 2,000 men.

There was a sudden shattering explosion as a gun opened fire on the Fort. They tried to see where it was, but it was well hidden in the trees, and kept the defenders under cover with an occasional shot at the Fort.

From his position Joseph could see a large number of men moving about and flitting between the trees, around rocks, taking advantage of every form of cover, but slowly making their way towards the Fort.

"They're trying to take the Fort from the land side!" he bellowed. "Line up the musket men and fire down at them. Throw a barrage of grenades and give them something to remember."

The musket men ran to their positions and came into their own as they fired down at the elusive figures. Other men tossed grenades which burst amongst the invaders, several of whom threw up their hands and spun round to fall to the ground; some lay still, others writhed with the agony of their wounds, trying to crawl to shelter away from the devastating hail of lead, leaving bloodstained trails in their wake.

A messenger came panting up to the Commandant to give the alarming message that the enemy ship, which had drifted out of sight around the corner, had been stranded on a sandbank opposite the small Fort Joseph which guarded the harbour entrance. This was out of range of the guns of the main

Fort, and after several shots, the enemy had landed a party which had attacked the small Fort and had overwhelmed it. Some of the defenders had escaped after a fierce battle and were now waiting until dark to try and join the main force in Fort Jesus. Their guns had been captured and these were the guns which were firing at the Fort from the shelter of the trees, where the enemy had dragged them.

More messages came into the Fort and it was found that the town and island had been quietly occupied by the enemy. Various reports put the numbers of invaders at between 2,000 and 3,000 men.

At the end of the first day's fighting, the enemy, although occupying most of the island and the town, were unable to make any impression on the Fort. In fact, the firing of the muskets and grenades from the Fort had claimed many victims and now the enemy had withdrawn to a safe distance.

A strong guard was mounted at the Fort, with sentries watching every vulnerable point, but their vigilance was needless; the enemy had retreated to lick their wounds.

Soon darkness descended and there was silence.

Chapter 7

Inside the Fort, however, a meeting was in progress, for the Commandant had called his officers together.

"Now is the time to counter-attack and put the stolen guns out of action," he said with a frown. "They've already caused several casualties and, if they're allowed to continue firing tomorrow, they'll certainly cause more. Have any of you gentlemen any suggestions to make as to how we can best carry out this task?"

"Yes, Sir!" the Moor spoke up. "Let me lead a squad of picked men through the tunnel and we'll guarantee to silence the guns – and the men firing them."

No other suggestion was made, so Captain Mogo de Mello called for a party of volunteers from amongst the gunners. Leonardo Nunes came forward with five other men, all tough, seasoned fighters and wise in warfare.

At last the small party was ready and the Captain inspected them. They had rubbed burnt cork over their faces and hands and wore dark clothing. They all carried daggers and grenades in their belts and it is doubtful whether even their own mothers would have recognised them!

"Let's go, men!" The Moor raised his hand and his men followed him. He went down a passageway and stepped into a small store. "The ammunition store!" he whispered in answer to one of the men. Pulling aside a few timbers, he revealed a hole behind a false wall. This wall was so cunningly made that only someone who knew the secret would be able to find it.

"Keep all knowledge of this to yourselves," the Captain warned the men, as he lead them through the hole into a passage carved out of the coral rock. "It's a dangerous secret, but one I'm forced to share – but I trust you all, for your lives are at stake too!"

They carried on for some distance along the passage, which was so low that the taller men had to keep their heads bent, until it divided into two forks.

"This route takes us to Fort Joseph. The other one goes down to the beach, just under the Fort," de Mello explained quietly.

They all crept after him again as he went on for a while, then he stopped and said, "There are two forks again now. One would take us direct to Fort Joseph and the other one takes us just behind it; the last is the better route as it takes us immediately behind the guns which we want to destroy. Follow me very quietly," he went on, "and when we reach the guns, you know what to do!"

Then he lead them out of a cave in the cliff, the entrance of which was hidden behind a bush.

Slowly and painfully they made their way quietly through the undergrowth until at last they could see the shapes of the guns faintly in the pale glimmer of moonlight; they could also see the outlines of five men guarding them.

"Try and kill them without raising the alarm," the Captain whispered as they crouched watching the men in front of them.

The enemy were quite oblivious of their presence; so much so that one man even wandered towards them and urinated into the bushes nearby before wandering back to join his fellows. The others were half asleep, staring into the darkness ahead.

"Now!" hissed the Moor, and one by one his men slipped quietly away, each to his appointed task. Five of the men slid forward and the two waiting men saw the five guards soundlessly slip to the ground as, simultaneously, a hand clapped over their mouths and a dagger slipped between their ribs. De Mello's men had done their deadly work both soundlessly and well!

"Our turn now!" the Moor whispered to Leonardo Nunes. They made their way to the guns, and between them damaged them to such an extent that they could never be fired again.

"If anyone tries to fire these now," Nunes whispered with a grim chuckle, "he'll blow himself and his friends to Hell!"

Their work over, the small party retraced their steps, being careful to hide all marks of their passing. Within an hour: they were safely back in the Fort, reporting their success to the Commandant, who heartily congratulated them.

In the meantime the four Portuguese officers and 250 Swahili soldiers from Fort Joseph had been admitted under cover of darkness to the big Fort.

It had been a good night's work and the defences of the Fort would benefit by it.

Chapter 8

For the next eight days those who were under siege in the Fort were in a state of preparedness and yet, apart from the enemy beating drums, blowing war horns and letting off occasional shots, all was fairly quiet.

The days were long and hot – and the soldiers, who normally could relax without their leather jerkins, felt the heat badly. Indeed, a couple of the older men had died from heat stroke, and the room where the women were treating the sick was becoming increasingly crowded. The fetid, stale atmosphere became worse in spite of a fan they had made by suspending pieces of wet cloth from a frame, which was pulled by a boy. This had the effect of moving the stale, hot air around, and bringing an illusion of coolness to the suffering men.

The heat got on everyone's nerves and discipline had to be harsh to keep down the fights and quarrels resulting from the tense situation.

The nights were the worst. The moon was full and sentries had to be relieved frequently as they began to see and hear all sorts of things which existed only in their own imaginations.

One man, who had been behaving in a peculiar manner for days, started foaming at the mouth and shouting, "Stop those drums! Stop those drums!"

He broke frantically away from the men who were trying to hold him. Then, with panting breath and staring eyeballs, he ran to the edge of the parapet, where he hesitated a moment before leaping over – to fall screaming onto the rocks below. His twisted body lay still.

This dismal scene caused a mood of depression to settle like a dark cloud over the Fort, so the Commandant, who had been ill himself from overwork, worry and fever, decided to call a conference of his officers. As they filed into his quarters, he sat in his chair wrapped in his cloak for, in spite of the heat, he was shaking from fever. His officers sat on chairs near him and he spoke to them in a tired voice.

"Gentlemen," he said, "our situation is very serious. We are at the moment holding our own against the enemy, who surrounds us in vastly superior numbers, but we have many mouths to feed and our stores and supplies will not last many months at the present rate of consumption, even with rationing. We will need more stores and ammunition. As you know, many of our men have already been struck down by illness and our medical supplies are insufficient for a long siege.

"It is not long since the supply ships left and they're not due back for another year, so it's essential that we get help and get it fast, for our people don't know of our danger. Someone will have to go for help! This isn't going to be easy, for it means leaving the safety of the Fort and risking capture by the enemy. It means sailing in a small boat, often against the south wind; escaping the notice of the enemy and making for Zanzibar and Mozambique to warn our friends, the Queen of Zanzibar and the Commandant of the Fortress at Mozambique, of our predicament.

"This is such a dangerous mission that I will not order any one of you gentlemen to go, but ask for a volunteer. Captain de Britto I can see the eager look in your eye, but I can't permit you or any of my other senior officers to volunteer. You are of the utmost importance to the safety of the Fort. The volunteer will have to be one of my junior officers. Gentlemen?"

There was a silence as he finished speaking – each man was busy with his thoughts – then almost as a man the younger officers stood up to show they were willing to go.

Rodrigues Leao looked at them each in turn and then said gravely, "There are five of you, gentlemen – only one can go! May I suggest that you cut cards to decide who will be the one to undertake this dangerous journey?"

There was immediate agreement, so, opening a drawer in the table at his side, the Commandant took a pack of cards. He shuffled them and said, "Gentlemen, the one who picks the Ace of Diamonds will be the one to go."

The atmosphere in the room grew tense as the five young men gathered around the Commandant's chair. He held out a fan of cards to each of them in turn and they picked a card from the spread held before them. One or two foreheads were damp with sweat as they hesitated to look at the pieces of cardboard. They turned the cards over and either gave a sigh of relief or disappointment, according to their nature. Nine times the Commandant held out the cards for them to choose, but still the vital card had not been drawn. There were seven cards left in his hand.

Only the sound of breathing broke the tense silence in the room as the Commandant handed out the last cards.

This time the eyes of one of the young men lifted to meet those of the Commandant.

"I go, Sir!" Jose Barraso spoke quietly.

He had felt fear and his heart lurched as he turned each card in turn, until finally his damp hands had turned over the last card he had drawn, the Ace of Diamonds! This then was to be his testing time! He drew himself up proudly, stepped up to the Commandant and saluted. "I'm ready for your orders, Sir". He spoke formally and waited while the other young officers were dismissed to go about their duties. Then he was invited to sit down with the senior officers while they set about making plans for his departure the next night, the 20th of March.

It was pitch dark. The moon was on the wane and only the faint light of the stars enabled Jose to make out the shape of a small boat as it lay alongside the jetty, at the water gate below the Fort.

The enemy were near – he could see their fires and even, faintly, hear their voices, but they didn't appear to have any sentries out, and Jose, six Swahili boatmen and one of the Portuguese soldiers who could speak fluent Swahili, felt their way cautiously down to the jetty. This was very difficult in the dark as they were loaded with food, water and arms.

The boat had been lying under the jetty for several weeks and the bottom held several inches of water. However, they dared not risk bailing out now and could only stow their stores on the seats as far as possible away from the salt water. They had also brought sails and oars with them, and these were stowed in the front of the boat.

Jose wrapped his dark cloak closer around himself and pulled his helmet low over his face, then took his place in the boat. In a short time they were all safely on board, and it only remained to push away from the jetty slowly and make their way silently out of the harbour.

Suddenly they froze! They could hear voices approaching. Jose whispered to the men to remain very quiet and they all crouched down and sat as still as possible.

The voices came closer and soon the men in the boat could hear what they were saying. They were talking about fishing!

"This jetty is a good place at night," said a deep voice. "I caught a big one here three nights ago."

"No, *rafiki yangu*," said a higher-pitched voice. "It's better that we go on to the jetty near the town. The fish are more plentiful there for they are attracted by the food the soldiers throw into the water from the ships."

They stood arguing for a short time, while the men sitting in the boat below them hardly dared to breathe. At last the man who favoured fishing from the town jetty managed to persuade his friend to go there as the lights would attract more fish. The two voices faded away into the distance as the men walked away.

The men in the boat kept quiet for another few minutes, then Jose said quietly, "Phew! That was close! Come on, men, let's go!" They quietly pushed the boat away from the side of the jetty and let the current take them into the middle of the channel. They dared not use the sail as it would be seen as a white blur in the starlight but they used the oars which had been muffled to deaden any sounds.

They rowed for about an hour, with brief pauses to rest. At last they were clear of the harbour and out at sea. Jose then gave the order, "Hoist the sail", and at last they set off southwards and were lucky enough to have a good breeze behind them.

Their journey was to be a long one, and it was nearly five months before Jose Barraso and his companions saw the Fort again.

Chapter 9

Easter had come at the end of April, and with it a few showers of rain. Father Antonio, more comfortable now the cooler weather had brought him relief from his prickly heat, had just celebrated the festival in the Chapel. He was beginning to notice the gaps in his congregation, but did his best to comfort the sick and dying and keep the living cheerful.

He tried to organise lessons for the younger people, and Carlos and Hussein found themselves going to the Priest's quarters daily with a few other children. They enjoyed their lessons, for the good father made them as interesting as he could, telling them little anecdotes and legends of his past in Portugal. They learned the lives of the Saints, without realising that the man who taught them was himself a saint in his own way.

Father Antonio often went to spend an evening with the Commandant, who was a good friend of his. They used to sit for hours playing chess, but sometimes the talk would come round to Carlos and his future.

"If anything happens to me, will you do me the honour of becoming Carlos' guardian, Father Antonio?" asked the Commandant one evening as the men sat quietly talking.

"Although I pray that such a day is far off, my friend," Father Antonio replied, "I'll be honoured to accept your charge. I love the boy, for haven't I watched him grow and develop from the time he was born, and did I not hold him in my arms to baptise him before we had even left Goa? I'll see that he lacks nothing

– but I pray you'll live a long life and that it will be many years before I have to take on my charge."

Rodrigues Leao sat looking at the lamp in silence for a long time; then he said hesitatingly, "It's a peculiar thing, Father, but recently I've been dreaming a lot of my beloved wife and I often hear her calling me."

"It's probably the effect of the fever!" the Priest said. "It can make a man imagine all sorts of things."

Rodrigues shook his head emphatically. "No!" he said, "I know that I won't live very long. I'm not a young man; I'm over fifty and I've led a very hard life. My happiness ended when my dear wife died, and although I love my son dearly, I'm not sorry to feel that my time is coming to depart from this life. You know in your heart that I speak the truth, Father. I'm a sick man and these attacks of fever are becoming more frequent. I'll carry on as long as I'm given strength, for it's my duty; but when the time comes for me to die, I'll say farewell without regrets – especially now I've your promise to care for Carlos."

These were the days when men lived in the shadow of death, and the Priest knew his friend had spoken the truth. Rodrigues Leao was a very sick man and it was only his great will-power that kept him alive. He forced himself daily to get up and inspect the Fort and to see to the comfort of his people. But the Priest could see that he was daily growing weaker.

Fortunately, he was able to hand over a lot of the routine administrative work of the Fort to his Captains, Antonio Mogo de Mello and Joseph de Britto. The two young Arab princes were also given the rank of Captain.

Chapter 10

The heat reached its peak in mid-April and some showers fell, cooling the air for a few hours before the heat began again, but in May the rains really set in. The sky was grey and overcast and water fell out of the heavens as though a huge sluice gate had been opened. The relief from the heat was almost immediate; but the onset of the rains brought other problems, for water lay in pools around the Fort. The harsh incessant croaking of frogs rose to disturb people's sleep, and the nights were made hideous by the buzzing of mosquitoes and other insects.

Centipedes, scorpions and snakes now appeared in large numbers, and there were several casualties and nasty bites and stings, especially among the children, who were curious and would poke their feet or fingers at anything to see what would happen.

A severe period of illness amongst the garrison commenced, and the plight of the people camped in the moat was pitiful. Every day or so both the Catholic and Muslim priests had to bury one or two people. Strange to say, the children seemed to have more resistance than the adults, and it was the older people who succumbed first.

Maria and her mother had been spending most of their time nursing the sick, of whom there were now very many. Maria sometimes managed to get a couple of hours to herself in the evenings and would often make her way to the ramparts where she could get a glimpse of the mouth of the harbour and enjoy the fresh air after the staleness of the sickroom.

The scene before her was quiet and outwardly peaceful. Across the water she could see a stretch of white sand, with low coral cliffs, a few palm trees and green vegetation growing near the water's edge.

In spite of the beauty of the scene, however, she knew that the wily Musungulos were lying in wait on the mainland for any unwary traveller, be he Portuguese or Omani.

The Musungulos were said to be descendants of the fierce Zimba warriors who had swept their way up from the south nearly a hundred years ago. They attacked and pillaged towns and villages, and terrorised the frightened inhabitants, until at last they were badly defeated by the Sheikh of Malindi, aided by the Mosseguejos in 1589.

Maria shuddered when she thought of them, for there had been several cases of men in boats being swept off course, and their dead bodies being washed up later on the beaches of the island.

Very often as she sat on her little stool in her favourite place under the shadow of a wall, out of the bright sunshine, in the pleasant cool breeze, she looked up from her sewing or reading to find Joseph de Britto's dark eyes smiling down at her. She would blush faintly but would make him welcome, and he would come and sit near her. He would talk and she would listen, for he was a well-educated man and widely travelled. Encouraged by her interest, he would tell her stories of life in Portugal and Goa.

Their growing friendship was observed, and approved, by her cousin, Prince Daud. He admired Joseph, who was a fine soldier, but was a man who could also meet him on his own ground as a scholar.

There was also another watcher, but this time one who was insanely jealous, although Maria had never given him the slightest encouragement. This was Pedro da Sa.

Pedro felt he must possess Maria at any price. He had mentally undressed her a thousand times and now burned to turn his dreams into reality. Maria, sensing his obsession from the way he looked lasciviously at her, disliked and distrusted him, and although outwardly polite when they met, she avoided him whenever possible. This was very difficult in the confines of the Fort, especially as the Captain used to take every opportunity he could to accost her. Her coolness only seemed to make him desire her more, and he was not content merely to speak with her, but would stand as close as possible in order to try and touch her arm, squeeze her shoulder or run his fingers lingeringly up her neck when he was alone with her. Maria would move angrily away from him, but in his vanity he imagined she was just being provocative, and this spurred him to greater efforts to force his unwanted attentions on her.

One evening when she was sitting alone, Pedro da Sa sidled up to her and started to try and lead the conversation round to love.

"I love you, Maria, and dream of holding your soft, white body in my arms!" he declared passionately. As it was dusk, he put his arm around her.

Maria immediately shrugged it off and rose from her seat.

"I must leave," she said sharply. "My mother is waiting for me."

Her tone inflamed his passion beyond all reason. He gave a low snarl deep in his throat, which made him sound like a mad animal, and as Maria turned to pick up her sewing, she felt his arms reaching round her from behind like steel bands, pinioning her so that she was helpless.

His hands pushed and tore at the front of her bodice, and the more desperately she struggled, the more persistent he became.

"I must have you, Maria!" he panted hoarsely; and pushing back her head, kissed her full on the lips. He bruised her mouth and his fingers were like iron.

Maria twisted her head away from him, but her resistance only made him more ardent. Her breath came in gasps and she was crying with fear and anger.

"Leave me alone you beast," she panted. "I hate you! Let me go at once!" she cried as she struggled against his grip.

Savagely, he wrenched at the bodice of her gown, ripping it down to the waist, and his hands were at once pawing at her exposed breasts. Maria screamed and at once his hand covered her mouth and stifled her. She bit hard and could feel the salty taste of blood on her tongue.

"You bitch!" he growled in fury. "I'll kill you for that! If I can't have you, then no-one else will!"

He swung back his hand and hit her across the head. She moaned. Then seizing her throat in his large fleshy hands, he began to squeeze.... Maria was dazed, everything swam round and round and started turning black.

There was a sudden movement and da Sa was wrenched violently backwards and found himself looking into the blazing eyes of Joseph de Britto. He had been on his way to sit with Maria, when he had heard her terrified screams and to his horror had seen her struggling with da Sa. Immediately unsheathing his sword, he ran to her rescue, but was too late to prevent da Sa hitting her.

"On guard, you filthy dog!" he shouted. Pedro da Sa let go of Maria, bared his teeth in a snarl and, drawing his sword, rushed at Joseph.

Maria crept to the side of the ramparts, where she supported herself sobbing and half-fainting. Clutching together the torn edges of her bodice, she watched the men as they fought fiercely and silently. The only sound was their heavy breathing as they swayed to and fro.

Suddenly Maria gasped with horror as Joseph slipped and fell to one knee, but almost at once he was on his feet again, guarding himself before his opponent had time to give more than a triumphant grin.

Backwards and forwards they fought. Both were good fighters and fairly evenly matched, but da Sa was an older man and heavier and at last his age and weight began to tell and he became careless.

He thrust at Joseph and once succeeded in ripping his sleeve and drawing blood. He made a fatal mistake, however, and lowered his guard for a few seconds. Joseph was quick to seize his advantage and plunged the blade of his sword into his opponent's chest. Da Sa gave a choking cry and fell, mortally wounded.

Joseph ran to Maria and took her tenderly in his arms. "Are you all right, my darling?" he asked her anxiously.

Her only reply was a choking sob. He gently wrapped his cloak around the weeping girl and escorted her to her mother, who was just preparing the evening meal in their quarters.

Hadija went pale when she saw her daughter's condition.

"In the name of God! Whatever's the matter?" she gasped, horrified. "What's happened to Maria? Is she hurt? Who did this?" The questions came tumbling out, even as Hadija put her arms around her weeping daughter to comfort her. Joseph briefly explained what had happened, then left Maria in her mother's care. Gradually in the warm comfort of her mother's arms Maria's weeping stopped.

"Lie down, my dear one," Hadija said gently and when Maria obeyed, she covered her with a rug. She left her for a moment as she made up a sleeping draught, then she held her arm behind Maria's head and helped her to sit up and drink it.

"Close your eyes now and try and rest, you'll be all right now. It's been a nasty shock." Hadija sat next to her daughter's bed and stroked her forehead. She spoke to her softly until eventually her eyelids drooped and she fell asleep.

In the meantime Joseph went straight to the Commandant's quarters and knocked boldly at the door. "Come in!" a voice called out and he entered the room.

The Commandant had heard about the fight and listened gravely to Joseph's story.

Then he said, "There's no blame whatever attached to you, Captain de Britto, for you were defending Maria from a madman. It's no crime to have killed the cowardly da Sa for he was like a rabid dog, and he was killed in fair combat. You were merely protecting the honour of a young girl and you had no alternative. It was a case of killing him or being killed yourself. He was a thoroughly bad character anyway and we're well rid of him. We can only thank God that you arrived in time to protect Maria!"

The incident was soon forgotten by those in the Fort, but it made a big difference between Maria and Joseph who grew daily closer together.

Chapter 11

There was no sign of the enemy for several weeks, and although the defenders of the Fort knew they were still there, they seemed to be kept under cover by the heavy rain which continued to fall throughout May and June. The rain slackened off in July, but was replaced by strong winds from the southeast; this made life miserable during July and August, for it was cold and grey with overcast skies.

The trees no longer glistened in the sun or shone with a thousand rainbow tinted raindrops, but now swayed and shuddered in the gusts and flurries of wind which swept the island.

In Fort Jesus life went on much the same. Men died frequently now and the Priest and nurses were kept busy. However the discipline was strict and morale was kept high.

The evening of the 8th of August came, and as the sun set, there was a sudden excited cry of "Sails!" from the lookout. The watchers on the towers saw the sails of three ships in the distance coming along from the south. They were too far off to distinguish to whom they belonged, and only visible from the highest watch towers of the Fort. As darkness fell they disappeared from view.

That evening, soon after 9 o'clock they heard the sounds of a fight coming from below the gate. The alarm was given, and shouting "To the rescue!" a small party headed by Joseph rushed out of the gates.

They saw men in Portuguese uniform being attacked by Omanis and, with a shout of "At them, men!" Joseph and his followers at once joined in the fray. There was a brisk fight and soon the assailants were driven off. Jose Barraso had arrived back at the Fort!

"Help me to get the ships unloaded before they come back with reinforcements," he gasped to Joseph, who at once took charge of the situation and shouted orders.

Jose's arm was red with blood where the blade of one of the enemy had cut into it, but he disregarded the wound. Soon willing hands had made short work of unloading the stores and the much needed medical supplies; in less than an hour the great gate had been shut and bolted with the welcome reinforcements and stores safely inside the Fort. There were 28 Portuguese troops, 48 Swahili troops, five Swahili youths and a number of Zanzibari sailors.

Jose Barraso had succeeded in sailing down the Coast to Zanzibar, and from there had continued on to Mozambique, where the Governor had given him the soldiers and some supplies, with the promise of more help to come. They were expecting the fleet to arrive soon from Goa and would then send more help.

Jose was very tired after his long and hazardous journey, and his arm hurt a lot; as soon as he had reported to the Commandant, he was taken to the officers' quarters, his wound was dressed, he was given a meal and then went straight off to bed.

"Let him tell us the story of his adventures when he's recovered," the Commandant ordered. "He must rest now."

Carlos and Hussein were excited. The Fort had been dull and boring the last few weeks and, like all boys, they thrilled at the idea of adventure. Everyone waited eagerly for Jose Barraso to recover sufficiently to be able to tell his story.

A few evenings later Jose sat in the Commandant's quarters surrounded by eager, interested faces. He was thin and his lean, brown face had taken on a new maturity. His arm rested in a sling.

He looked around the room and saw the Commandant, looking pale and sick, sitting in his great chair next to his friend, Father Antonio. Mogo de Mello sat on his own – his great brooding eyes fixed on Jose.

Maria and Joseph sat together and, as the story unfolded, his hand crept out and clasped hers.

The young officers sat together. There were only two of them now – one had died of fever and another was being cared for in the makeshift hospital. Amongst the men who had arrived with Jose was a doctor; this was a great relief to Father Antonio, who had been trying to do the job to the best of his ability for the past few months. This officer sat next to the two young men.

Jose looked around at the familiar faces, and gave a smile in the direction of the two small boys seated in the corner of the room with the Prince of Faza, Prince Daud and Hadija. Then, at a nod from the Commandant, he began his tale. . . .

Chapter 12

"To begin at the beginning." Jose said, "I shall go back to the evening the Commandant commissioned me to go for help. I was nervous and apprehensive; but at the same time very proud to have been given this chance of proving myself. Knowing there was no time to be lost the Commandant at once called a meeting of the Senior Officers; as some of you know, plans were made for me to leave the next evening as soon as darkness had fallen.

"One of our Swahili men slipped out of the Fort to confirm that the boat was still lying hidden under the jetty, where we could reach it easily the following evening.

"We were busy the next day making up our provisions into small bundles, which would be easy for us to carry. We filled a couple of small barrels with water and took a little ammunition. We could not take very much, for the stores at the Fort had to be conserved, but we hoped to be able to replenish our stocks when we reached Zanzibar or Mozambique.

"When darkness had fallen, we were let quietly out of the small gate at the bottom of the tunnel which leads to the jetty. I wore my armour and ordered Miguel, who came with me, to do the same; but over that we wore dark cloaks and kept our helmets pulled low to hide our white faces.

"The guide was waiting there to show us where the boat had been hidden. We walked silently, in single file, behind him, and having pulled the boat out of its hiding place, quietly loaded everything into it.

"We were just preparing to push off when we thought our whole trip would be a failure. We heard voices approaching and a couple of men came up and held a discussion just above the place where we lay crouched in the boat. We tried to hold our breath for as long as we could.

"Eventually they moved off, and after a short wait we put out the muffled oars, and when the current had carried us to the centre of the creek, we started rowing. The tide was going out and this helped to carry us out to sea. It was pitch dark, so we were not seen from the shore. Once we were safely away from the harbour, we put up our sail and headed south.

"We sailed before the wind for many miles until at last the blackness of the night gave way to grey; then the sun came up over the horizon, deepening the sky to rose and gold, and finally turning it to a bright blue.

"It began to get hot, and as we had kept close to the shore during the night, we decided to land and find food and water, and have a rest. Our guide knew this coast well and told us that around the next headland we would find a small village where the people were friendly and would give us food and shelter.

"The sea sparkled, and looking down over the side of the boat as we turned towards the shore, we could see gaily coloured fish swimming amongst the coral ridges. The water was clear, cool and green and even the shells at the bottom could be seen clearly, although it was still very deep.

'There's the beach,' said our guide.

"Soon the little boat grounded on the sandy beach and we jumped out. We pulled it out of the water and up onto the sand just above the high tide mark; there we hid it in the thick bushes. The guide and one of the crew went off to see if they could find the village, while the rest of us swept the sand over the track made by the boat.

"We posted two guards, and then sent one of the men up a tree to cut down some coconuts. We prised off the thick outer husk with a sharpened stick, then using a sharp knife, sliced off the top of the nut and quenched our thirst with the cool liquid inside.

"Soon we heard the men returning from the village. They brought several others with them. These men were dressed in long white robes, dark waistcoats with fancy embroidery, and small round white hats. They were Swahilis, and had a very grave and dignified demeanour. One of them was introduced as the Chief of the village and another as the Priest; the rest were elders. After greeting us, they offered us the hospitality of their village, which we accepted gladly. They then told us to follow them.

"Leaving two of our men guarding the boat, we followed the Swahilis back to the village. We walked along a path which wound through the palm trees, passed a well where women were drawing water, and eventually arrived at a collection of huts made of mud and coral, and roofed with a thick thatch of woven palm leaves.

"Our hosts showed us into one of the huts, which we were told was kept for guests of the Chief. The room was dark and cool; against the walls stood beds of wood with leather thongs laced so as to form a soft spring; a cotton mattress lay on the top, with a finely woven mat over that. There were also pillows on the beds and they looked so comfortable that it did not take us long to strip off our shirts and fling ourselves down to rest. The men guarding our boat on the beach were relieved every two hours. The rest of us slept.

"When the sun started to go down it was much cooler. A messenger arrived from the Chief inviting us to eat with him that evening. I had wanted to push on, but it would have been taken as an insult to his hospitality to refuse to eat with him. I got up, washed and dressed and then, accompanied by Miguel, was escorted to a house larger than the others, standing in its own clearing.

"We were greeted by the Chief, dressed in spotless robes, standing at the door of his house."

"*Karibu*, he said.

"Then after an exchange of greetings, he led the way into a large room spread with carpets and cushions.

"*Keti*, he said, gesturing towards the cushions.

"We sat down and made ourselves comfortable, and in a short time steaming bowls of rice and meat were placed in the centre of the room and the Chief invited us to eat.

"It did not take us long to learn how to use our right hands for picking up the food, which is the customary way of eating in these parts, and we made a very good meal, for the meat was spiced and very tasty. Eventually, when we had eaten our fill, the dishes were cleared away and bowls were placed before us. We held our hands over the bowl and a small boy poured water over them until they were clean, then he handed us small towels.

"Then more bowls arrived with various fruits and sweetmeats and we were given the fresh juice of oranges and coconuts to drink. After our meal we sat back, replete, to enjoy some sweet black coffee served in tiny cups. Then we began to talk.

"The Chief asked us about the invasion of the Omani and said that the news of the siege had spread even to the remote inland villages. Most of the villages along the coast were governed by Swahili and Arab chiefs. They were not in sympathy with the Sultan of Oman and lived in fear of his soldiers, so we could count on help from the people along our way.

'You must make for Bagamoyo,' he said, looking at us gravely. 'From there it's but a short trip to Zanzibar. When you get close to Bagamoyo, however, you must take the utmost precaution, for we've heard that the town is already in the hands of the Omani, and they'll have no mercy on you.

"'As you're white men you must disguise yourselves as Swahilis,' he went on. 'For should you have the misfortune to fall into the hands of the enemy, you may be able to pass as traders. We can let you have suitable clothing and will help to disguise you. Your armour will only draw attention to the fact that you're Portuguese.'

"He drew us a map of our route and also gave us the names of the villages where we would be sure of receiving food and shelter along the coast. It was, he added, wise for us to travel only by night as then there was less likelihood of capture by enemy ships.

"He finally advised us to rest as much as possible the next day, and said he would send men with food and water to the boat. We could then leave at sunset in the evening. I thanked the good Chief for his help and advice and we were escorted back to the hut, where we went gladly to rest.

"The next morning was spent in putting our boat in order for the long trip ahead of us; and again we rested during the heat of the afternoon. By sunset everything had been prepared. By this time, Miguel and I were dressed as Swahilis and had dyed our skins dark with some liquid the Chief had given us, so we could have passed for Arabs. Our understanding and ability to speak Swahili was improving greatly. Two of us were Christians, but we learned to copy the movements of the Muslims at prayer, as this was an important part of Swahili life; being unable, or unwilling, to pray would have betrayed us at once to the enemy had we fallen into their hands.

"The Chief and the Priest accompanied us to the boat when the time came for us to leave. They raised their hands in farewell as we pushed off, and as the breeze caught the sail, we heard them call out softly '*Assalaam aleikum*'. Then we saw them turn and make their way back to the village as we sailed off in the fading light."

Chapter 13

Jose Barraso paused in his narrative to take a drink of wine as his throat felt dry with the unaccustomed talking. Then, having refreshed himself, he continued his tale:

"For several weeks we travelled down the coast, always taking care to seek shelter at dawn. We sometimes landed on deserted beaches and had to fend for ourselves, but at other times we landed at the small fishing villages the Chief had told us about, and were invariably made welcome and given food and shelter. At last we came to the vicinity of Bagamoyo and began to move with even greater caution.

"One day our guide told us we would reach the village before Bagamoyo the following day. He advised us to wait and try and find out the latest news of the movements of the Omani.

"Just before dawn the guide pointed to a spot on the beach and said, 'The village is about half a mile from the beach. We must land here and hide the boat safely.'

"Exercising the greatest caution, we hid the boat in some mangroves and waded ashore, taking advantage of every bit of cover on the way. It was just as well we did so!

"All at once there arose a great shouting and screaming and we saw flames and smoke rising into the sky ahead of us. We kept cautiously on and, peering through the bushes, we saw a dreadful sight!

"The village which was our destination, had just been attacked by a band of Omani slave traders and set on fire; they were now proceeding to sack it. All the old people had been rounded up together with the very tiny babies, and were being butchered to the accompaniment of screams of anguish from their people. Some of the old people tried to run, but were cut down by the Omanis; others were thrown alive into the roaring flames. Tiny babies were torn from their weeping mothers' arms and decapitated before being flung into the flames. Their frenzied shrieks rang loudly above the sound of the crackling fire, and shouts and screams of the other villagers. It was like a scene in Hell!

"We watched this pitiful slaughter in terror, unable to assist them in any way as there were too many of the enemy and, had we gone to their aid, we would soon have been overpowered. The slavers, who were laughing and joking amongst themselves, then began to round up the captives. They herded the women together. Then they separated the young girls from the older women, tearing the men away who were trying to protect them. The village was by now a smoking ruin and there were dead and dying people scattered all over the open space in the centre.

"The captives were now herded into rows, where the slavers put wooden yokes around their necks and chained them together. Some of the men who had put up a fight had chains fastened around their ankles so that they could only shuffle along painfully. The slavers and their servants ran up and down the rows of people with whips, lashing out at those who cried out, or showed any signs of struggling or fighting.

"A long procession was formed and we had the agony of watching them shuffling off – weeping captives! The village was razed to the ground, and the dead and dying lay ready for the vultures, which were already gathering in the trees above.

"We watched the dismal scene with the utmost horror, unable to move. We had all heard of the evil slavers, but had never come in contact with them before.

"At last, when all was silent, we crept out of our hiding place and went to see if we could help any of the dying. They were all too far gone, with the exception of one young boy who had been cut down as he fought to save his old mother and had been left for dead. He had had the sense to close his eyes and hold his breath when any of the enemy went near him, and they were so intent on herding together the fit captives that they did not trouble with those they thought were dead.

"We found the boy was alive and attended his wounds. He then asked in a weak voice for water, which we gave him. As he had now appeared to have slightly recovered, we asked him what had happened. He then told us his story in a barely perceptible whisper.

"'We were just preparing to go out fishing for the day,' he said. 'Some of the men hadn't even left their huts as it was hardly light. The women were busy over their cooking pots while the children played in the dust in front of the doors; all was quiet and peaceful and the first we knew of a raid was the sound of guns being fired and people shouting. Taken by surprise as we were, it was not easy to put up a fight and any who showed resistance were killed instantly. The raid had been carefully planned, for the village was entirely surrounded by the slavers' men, who now moved in and set our huts on fire straight away, thus further confusing us. We had no chance and had you arrived a few moments earlier, you too would have been captured or would have perished. Oh! my poor people!' and turning his face away, he wept bitterly.

"Wasting no more time on the desolate scene, we carried him to where our boat was concealed and there hid ourselves under a large bush for the rest of that day. At last, when the sun went down, we set the sail and were soon heading out to sea.

"We all discussed the matter and decided not to attempt any more landings until we reached Zanzibar. We knew the direction of the island and should, with luck, land there within two or three days.

"We sailed on through the night and when the sun rose, the land was out of sight. However, we had a chart, and used the sun by day and the stars by night to guide us.

"It was very hot in the boat and the young boy became feverish from his wounds. He told us his name was Hassani. We built a little shelter over him to shield him from the sun, and eventually he dropped off into a doze, remaining more or less unconscious for the next two days.

"On the third day, in the early morning, we looked towards the horizon, and to our joy saw the shadow of the island of Zanzibar rising out of the morning mist; before evening we had reached the island."

Chapter 14

Once again there was a pause while Jose Barraso recovered from describing the terrible scenes which were still so vivid in his memory. Everyone was silent and after taking another sip of wine, he went on with his story.

"On beaching our boat, we were immediately surrounded by a crowd of curious onlookers, who thronged round us as we stepped ashore. Miguel at once asked one of the older men to escort us to the Queen of Zanzibar, and the man beckoned to us to go with him. Some of the crowd followed us through the narrow streets of the town. We passed overhanging balconies and great doors, made of intricately carved wood and studded with brass, until at last we reached the palace, where, after a short wait, Miguel and I were escorted in front of the Queen.

"The Queen was seated on a great throne of carved ebony, richly inlaid with gold and ivory; it was set on a beautiful carpet of glowing colours. She was heavily veiled, according to the custom of the high-born women of Zanzibar.

"She greeted us with a soft voice, and, then asked us the reason for our coming to her country. I bowed low, then told her our story, and begged her for her assistance. The Queen listened quietly and thoughtfully, her chin resting on her hand, then she spoke.

"'My friends, your plight moves me, for we too suffer from the depredations of the Omani and live in constant fear of attack. Alas, I have only a small force of fighting men and few ships, but I'll consult with my ministers and see what can be done to help you with ships, men and provisions. Rest with us a few days while we make preparation for your onward journey to Mozambique; there the big fort is manned by your own people, the Portuguese; I think they will be able to give you more help than we can with our limited resources.'

"The Queen then invited us to dine with her that evening. We thanked her, then as the interview appeared to be over, we bowed and left her presence.

"A servant, who had been standing outside the door, asked us to follow him and took us through the palace to a very comfortable room where we were to rest until evening. Water had thoughtfully been provided for washing, so we were able to clean off the dirt which had accumulated during the last few weeks of travelling. We then had a light meal of fruit and fruit juices, and lay on our beds to sleep; it was still early but we were both very tired.

"The sun was losing its heat when we were awakened by a servant who came softly into the room and pulled aside the shutters. He handed us clean robes and sandals and waited while we changed. While we were dressing, we inquired after the Swahilis who had been with us, and were told that they had been given accommodation in a different part of the palace and were being cared for by other Swahili people.

"Soon we were ready and followed the servant, who led us into a large, airy hall, where a feast had been prepared on low tables set at one end of the room. There were big, colourful cushions scattered about on beautiful carpets for us to sit on, and we could look out across a wide verandah towards the sea. A pleasant, cool breeze blew across in our direction.

"The Queen came into the room, followed by several men, who she introduced as her ministers. Then she bade us be seated. Although she sat amongst us, she did not have any food. She told us that it was not the custom in her country for men and women to eat together.

"She clapped her hands and the great doors opened to admit several servants carrying heaped dishes which they set in the centre of the tables. Dish after dish was put before us; great bowls of white steaming rice cooked in coconut milk, which gave it a very delicate flavour; rice fried with onions and flavoured with sticks of cinnamon and other spices. There were platters piled high with steaming meat, fish and poultry, which gave out most enticing odours. A whole sheep had been roasted and was served filled with rice, almonds, and fragrant spices.

"There were bowls of boiled and roasted grains and other vegetables and salads served in a variety of ways. The feast ended with piles of exotic sweetmeats and great bowls of fruit – mangoes, oranges, bananas, and passion fruit. We were given ice cold water and served with small cups of sweet black coffee. Finally we sank back replete against the cushions, and watched the entertainment provided for us, which consisted of musicians and dancers.

"Some of these dancers were young and beautiful and had carefully reddened their lips and cheeks with cosmetics, blackened their eyes and powdered their faces and necks. Their hair was long and shining and they tossed it around as they danced. They were very graceful and the small silver bells on their ankles and wrists tinkled in rhythm with the music. We were amazed when we were told afterwards that they were boys dressed up as girls, who had been trained as dancers from an early age.

"When the dancing came to an end, the Queen clapped her hands and, bidding us goodnight, told an attendant to show us to our rooms. We stood up, bowed to her and the other guests and took our leave.

"We remained in Zanzibar for six days while the ships were prepared for our onward voyage. We stayed on at the palace where we were royally entertained by the Queen. She was delighted to hear our tales of Mombasa, Goa and Portugal, and above all to hear about the customs and fashions of our Portuguese ladies.

"She told us sadly that the people of Zanzibar were afraid of invasion themselves, for they had been threatened by the Omani. They had already hidden their most precious jewellery and valuables and had many secret places prepared. These hideouts were so well stocked that people could survive in them for years if necessary.

"She went on to tell us about the slave trade, and of the pirates who ravished villages and stole ships all along the East African coast.

"'These pirates sail in long, low vessels which have projecting prows and sterns and very high rudder heads,' she informed us. 'They use this type of ship as they are very fast and easy to handle. The pirates are all expert seamen and completely fearless. Some of their ships have bowsprits curved like a camel's neck, and a white eye surrounded by a red ring decorating the prow. This, they believe, is the symbol of the Holy she-camel mentioned in the Holy Koran.'

"'What would they have done with the unfortunate people we saw them capture?' I asked the Queen.

"'Alas! Those people have a very slight chance of survival, for they are treated with the utmost cruelty which completely breaks their spirit, so that they long for death to relieve them of their misery.

"'When the slavers get them to the coast or loading places, they lay them in rows in the holds of their hell-ships. Two adults are placed with a child wedged between them or on top of them. A few inches above their heads is another layer of planks on which more unfortunate slaves are laid. These fiends continue loading the ship with layers of slaves and planks until it is full. Now and then they release their captives for food and air, for a sick slave fetches a poor price. This is the time the dead are collected from amongst the living and thrown overboard. Sharks always follow slave ships for they know they will be well fed! Our poor people on the mainland have suffered greatly from the Omani slavers!'

"I saw her eyes fill with tears, so I changed the subject and asked her to tell us some more about her lovely island, and she forgot her sorrow as she described the beautiful palm-fringed beaches, and her people, whom she loved deeply.

"When at last the time came for us to depart, we took our leave of the Queen, thanking her for her help and kindness. She made a little speech, wishing us 'Godspeed.'

"'My friends, your stay with us has passed swiftly and it is with sorrow we see you depart. Go with God. May the wind fill your sails so that you will soon return to Mombasa with your mission completed, and with help for your friends against the Omani. I fear we may not meet again in this life. God bless and preserve you!'

"'Madam,' I replied as I bowed deeply, 'our very grateful thanks are due to you for the hospitality and assistance you have given us in our hour of need. We will all pray for your continued health and safety. I can assure you that the gratitude and protection of the King of Portugal will be yours when he hears of the charity which you have meted out to his subjects. God keep you, Madam!'

"With this, we went down to our ships and prepared to set sail.

"The sailors pulled on the ropes – the sails rose high and we all waved to the watchers on the shore as we moved slowly out to sea. Soon the wind filled the sails of the three ships and Zanzibar faded into the distance as we sped on our way."

Chapter 15

"The ship the Queen had given us seemed very large in comparison with our boat, and when the wind filled the sails, she was very fast. Content with the knowledge that we were on our way once again, we sailed on in convoy for several peaceful days towards Mozambique.

"We saw porpoises and flying fish, and one day we sailed through a mass of jelly-fish. Huge fishes leapt out of the water, and once, in the distance, we saw the forms of three enormous whales, gambolling in the water.

"The weather began to get colder and white horses appeared on the tops of the waves. We had now entered the channel which would soon lead us to Mozambique.

"One night we were woken by a strong wind. In no time at all black clouds had covered the stars and the sea became so tough that high waves broke over the ship and drenched us. The lightning flashed and thunder crashed and rolled around us; rain followed, hissing and pouring down in almost solid sheets upon the decks. This lashing rain, coupled with the high seas and gusty wind, put us in danger of sinking.

"I shouted to the crew to lower our great sail and put out a sea anchor. Then, having done all I could, I sent up a prayer for help. This prayer was answered, for by God's grace, we rode out the storm, although it continued to roar and scream around us for the next two days.

"We were in a sorry state as we were all sick from the violent movement of the boat, and thanked God when the storm gradually blew itself out and we could see, to our joy, that the other ships were also safe near us. Soon we were all able to continue on our way once more, although the sea was still running very high. From this point our voyage went smoothly.

"On board the three ships we had, as well as the Mombasa crew, forty eight Swahili soldiers and the seamen from Zanzibar to aid us. We had left the boy Hassani in Zanzibar to recover from his wounds and had given him our little boat as a parting gift, little knowing under what circumstances we were to see him again.

"Early one morning we sighted Mozambique, and Miguel and I put on our armour in preparation for landing. Soon we were able to land and on explaining our mission to a group of soldiers who had come down to meet us, were immediately escorted into the presence of the Governor of the Fort, and explained the dangerous situation in Mombasa.

"The Governor stroked his beard as he listened to our story, but at the end he shook his head sadly and said, 'You come at a bad time, Captain Barraso, for my troops are depleted by illness and I am waiting for reinforcements from Goa. We have no ships to spare and I will only be able to send twenty eight men to assist you, although I would willingly give you more if I could. I can, however, help you with supplies of ammunition, and also with medical stores. In addition, I'll send a doctor with you. I give my word that as soon as the fleet arrives from Goa, relief will be sent to Fort Jesus.'

"Time was passing fast and we had no idea how our comrades in Mombasa were faring, so we urge the Governor to make all haste. He assured us he would do all in his power, and he kept his word, for he had everything ready and loaded onto our three ships within a week.

"As soon as everything was aboard, we bade our hosts farewell and started on our journey back to Mombasa. This time we travelled much faster for we had a following wind all the way. Soon we were approaching Zanzibar again, but this time we found that things were very different!

"As we came near the island, we saw a small boat bobbing about on the water and recognised it to be the one we had left behind in Zanzibar. As we drew alongside we found the boy, Hassani, and four companions.

"We helped them aboard and they told us that soon after our departure, the Omani had attacked Zanzibar, causing great loss of life and property and were now in complete control of the island. The Queen had escaped with her family and was safely in hiding. Hassani and his companions had made their way with danger and difficulty to the little boat, and had escaped from the island and had come to warn us not to land or we would undoubtedly be killed or captured by the Omani.

"On hearing this, we let the little boat go and made haste to sail away from Zanzibar. We sailed out of sight of land for several days until we came near the village where the chief had been so kind to us on the first day of our trip. We then guided our vessels close to the shore until at last we recognised the beach. There we anchored and leaving a strong guard on the ships, Miguel and I, accompanied by a few men, went to pay our respects to the Chief.

"The Chief was delighted to see us again and, after we had greeted each other, we warned him about the situation at Zanzibar. We then asked for news of the Fort at Mombasa, but the only thing he had heard was that the defenders were still holding out against the Omani hordes.

"We stayed overnight in the village as the guests of the Chief; the next day we said our farewells and set sail for Mombasa, timing it so that we would arrive after dark.

"We managed to get right up to the jetty bellow the Fort; but it was moonlight, and we were seen by a small group of the enemy as we landed, and had to fight our way to the Fort. This is the end of my story, for the rest you already know. I must add, however, that I am very glad to be back with you all safely after my wanderings."

Jose Barraso took out a large handkerchief and wiped his forehead as he sat down. There was silence for a short time, as his listeners thought over his story...then the Commandant spoke.

He praised the bravery of Jose Barraso and his men and said, "When I gave this mission to Captain Barraso, I had a few doubts, in view of his youth, as to his ability to carry it out successfully, but he has done so with honour, a sense of duty and much bravery. In spite of being the youngest officer in my command, he has certainly proved himself a man!"

Jose Barraso blushed scarlet as all his listeners stood up and cheered. They clapped him on the back and shook his hand and he felt terribly shy and embarrassed; but he was also very proud. He had been tried, and he had not been found wanting!

Chapter 16

Once the excitement of Jose Barraso's arrival had subsided, the life of the garrison began to take on its usual tempo, but the arrival of the reinforcements put new heart into them and a different spirit had entered the Fort; there was an air of optimism for the future.

The defenders now made several sorties out of the Fort and succeeded in securing the outside perimeter. The enemy, who had also suffered heavy losses from the plague, were forced to fall back beyond the town and soon fishermen and a few other traders were venturing to make their way by various means to trade with the Fort. For the first time for many months the inhabitants ate fresh fish, fruit, vegetables and meat. Once again they were able to replenish their stocks of food in case the Omani renewed their attacks.

Several of the merchants and their families now ventured to return to their dwellings in the town, where they felt they would be more comfortable and safer. They feared the plague which still carried off more victims in the Fort than the Omanis. The Commandant tried to warn them that this was probably a temporary lull in hostilities, but the merchants were determined to leave, so he let them go back to the town.

The medical situation had also improved; the new doctor was kept busy, but as well as the medical supplies brought in by the relief force, they were able to lay in a good stock of native herbs. Generally, the morale of the Fort was high at this period.

The night of the 20th of August followed a day like all the others; as dusk fell, the sentries were changed and the heavy gates were bolted and barred.

It turned out to be one of those inky-black nights, heavy with clouds and the threat of rain. It had been raining during the day, and the sentries were inclined to huddle under shelter as the wind howled and whistled around the wet stones of the fortress.

Joseph and Maria were sitting in a sheltered place near one of the bastions talking quietly together. Prince Daud saw them as he passed, and as he greeted them, thought what a handsome couple they made. He made his way unhurriedly to where his cousin, the Prince of Faza, was walking around the ramparts inspecting the sentries and joined him for a few moments conversation – all seemed quiet and peaceful!

However, as the two cousins were walking along the ramparts on the top of the bastion of St. Albert, they heard a scraping sound. On going to investigate, they saw to their horror that ladders had been placed silently against the lowest part of the defences, and that a strong party of the enemy were attempting to scale the walls. The sentry had been unable to shout a warning, for the enemy had crept on him silently from behind, and he was lying in a pool of blood with a dagger in his back.

Taking in the situation at a glance, the cousins drew their swords, at the same time shouting out at the top of their voices: "TO ARMS! TO ARMS! THE ENEMY ARE WITHIN THE FORT!" They ran up and down the ramparts cutting and slashing at heads and hands as they appeared over the top of the walls, and still shouting out "TO ARMS! TO ARMS! THE ENEMY ARE HERE!" as they ran.

The alarm rang out and shattered the peace and silence of the night. The clash of swords was heard as the defenders hurried to the walls. Joseph raced to assist the two Princes who were valiantly trying to stem the advance of the enemy over the parapets. The three of them were joined by other men-at-arms, and the former peaceful air was filled with the clash of metal; the thuds of bodies falling; the shouts, the curses and the screams of the wounded and dying.

As fast as the ladders were put against the walls, the enemy rushed up them in an attempt to climb into the Fort and take it by storm. The defenders were kept busy, slashing at the enemy and pushing the ladders away where they fell with their yelling hordes, crashing into the moat below the towering Fort. A few of the enemy succeeded in gaining the ramparts, and there was a desperate battle.

Joseph de Britto was cornered by a large Arab and was fighting for his life. Thrust, slash and parry – backwards and fowards they went, until at last the superior skill of the Captain showed, and he out-manoeuvered his enemy and ran him through. He pulled his sword out of the still body and stood panting as the bright blood dripped to the ground.

As he glanced around, he saw that a few of the enemy had penetrated the defences and had managed to sneak quietly into the Fort.

Maria had been standing where Joseph had left her when the alarm had sounded. She should have left and gone to safety with the rest of the women, but fear for her loved one made her forget the strict orders of the Commandant, and she remained rooted to the spot. She was so engrossed in watching the fighting that she failed to hear footsteps behind her and suddenly she felt herself seized by powerful arms, presumably to be used as a hostage.

She screamed – and her scream of quivering terror was heard by Joseph, who at once leapt to her rescue.

Quick as he was, however, there was one who was nearer and even quicker, her cousin, the Prince of Faza. He rushed into the centre of the struggling group, slashing and cutting with his sword. He ran his sword through the man who was holding Maria, and as the man's grip loosened, he shouted to her, "Run to safety, Maria. RUN!"

She obeyed him, and in spite of the efforts of some other men to catch her, she evaded them and escaped swiftly into the safety of the courtyard and ran to her mother, sobbing with fright.

In the meantime, Joseph and Prince Daud had come to the assistance of the Prince of Faza; but just as they battled their way to him, one of the enemy came up behind him and, raising his dagger, plunged it into the Prince's back. Prince Daud saw his cousin stagger, then recover himself and turn, at the same time running his sword through his assailant; then the young Prince collapsed and lay still on top of the body of his enemy.

The sounds of battle were growing less now; all the ladders had been thrown back from the walls, and the musket men had rushed up and were firing down and throwing grenades at the enemy, causing havoc and many casualties. The enemy now began to withdraw in disorder from the vicinity of the Fort, taking their dead and wounded with them. In the Fort there were no prisoners taken and the bodies of the invaders were thrown over the ramparts into the moat.

As silence fell, the Priest, the doctor and the women moved amongst the wounded and dying. When the casualties were accounted for, there were ten dead and many wounded.

Prince Mohamed of Faza regained consciousness and asked, "Is Maria safe?" before he was carried tenderly to his quarters, where Hadija and the doctor tried to cleanse his wound. It was useless, however, for the dagger had penetrated his lung, and he died before dawn with a smile on his lips for his aunt and cousins, who stood by his bedside.

Maria was distraught. "It's my fault! It's all my fault!" she cried over and over again, and her grief was inconsolable, for she felt responsible for her beloved cousin's death. Had she obeyed orders, she felt, he would not have died.

She retired sobbing bitterly into her room, supported by her anxious and sorrowing mother, who asked the doctor to give her a sleeping draught to give her peace and rest. By now Maria was quite hysterical and wild in her grief.

Joseph wanted to go to her, but Father Antonio put a restraining hand on his arm. "Let her weep and sleep," he counselled. "Tears are healing and so is sleep. She will still grieve, but will be better when she awakes. Your time will come to comfort her – but now is not the right time. Leave her to her mother who understands her!"

So Joseph went back to his duties of re-organising the defences of the Fort, with a heavy and anxious heart.

There was silence and mourning throughout the Fort, for Prince Mohammed of Faza had been beloved by all. The laughing Prince, as they had called him, was dead, and his cousin, Prince Daud, was now the new Prince of Faza according to the wishes of his people. Hussein was not chosen because he was still too young to bear the heavy responsibility, but he was the next in line for the title.

The Commandant had been among those wounded, and had a nasty gash in his arm. This was stitched and bound up, then he insisted, in spite of his illness and fever, and pain, in making a tour of the ramparts to inspect the defences himself. He was soon soaked through by the rain which now began to fall heavily, and it was only with the greatest difficulty that Antonio Mogo de Mello persuaded him to retire to his quarters and rest.

"You will be very ill if you carry on like this, Sir," he told him. "I can attend to all the routine matters and I promise to call you if an emergency should arise."

The rest of the night was quiet, and in the morning the sun shone on a sparkling world. The rain had gone and the sun rose in a clear, deep blue sky. The air was fresh and cool and had it not been for the shrouded figures of the dead and the silence of mourning in the Fort, the day would have seemed very beautiful. As it was, it made the death of the laughing, gallant Prince Mohammed much more poignant. He was only seventeen and at the threshold of his life; it was a tragedy for him to be cut down before he had really begun to live.

However, although the dead were mourned, the living had to go on, and in a couple of days the Fort was back to normal.

The enemy had definitely suffered the worst of the battle, for there was no further sign of them. Spies were sent out of the Fort and came back with stories that some of the big ships were being made ready for sea, and said that they had heard that the Omani Commander, Bir Ali, was leaving and was taking a lot of men with him, leaving only nine hundred on the island to watch the Fort.

These stories proved to be true, for early in the morning of the 25th of August, a lookout gave the alarm and the people saw six big ships sail out of the channel on the outgoing tide.

Hastily they fired several shots at them, but the range was too great. The enemy fired back at the Fort as they passed, but no damage was done. In no time their ships had caught the wind and were soon mere white specks on the horizon; eventually they dipped out of sight altogether.

Chapter 17

Spies soon reported that the remaining Omanis had gone to the other side of the island, so the defenders of the Fort gradually regained their confidence and began venturing outside the walls once more. Life was much more pleasant, and once again the mood of the Fort was one of cautious optimism.

After a few days, Maria reappeared; she looked pale and wan, but had recovered from the worst of her shock and grief for her cousin. Both Joseph and Prince Daud kept close by her side to distract her thoughts and amuse her; the three young people formed a close and lasting friendship.

Some of the very badly wounded and sick men had died and it was with sorrow that his people saw that the Commandant himself was also slowly sinking. He had worn himself out, and recurrent attacks of fever had so weakened him, that now he had no resistance to fight the infection of his wound.

He lived on for a few more weeks, growing daily weaker, and on the 23rd of October, two months after the raid on the Fort, he called for Father Antonio.

The good Father was soon at the bedside of the dying man and gave him Extreme Unction.

"Remember your promise!" Rodrigues Leao gasped, looking appealingly up at his friend.

The Priest gave him his hand to hold. "Peace, my friend! Carlos will be cared for," he said reassuringly, "and should anything happen to me, I have appointed Joseph de Britto as his guardian."

The dying man pressed his friend's hand in gratitude. Then Carlos was brought into the room to say goodbye to his father, who very shortly afterwards fell into a deep coma. He never awoke, but slipped quietly and peacefully away from his life on earth.

Carlos wept as Father Antonio gently covered his father's face. The Priest turned and put his arm round the boy's shaking shoulders.

"It's God's will, my son," he said quietly. "He was a gallant man. Remember, he's now with your Mother whom he loved so dearly!"

With the death of the Commandant, the command now fell on Antonio Mogo de Mello's capable shoulders, for he was the next senior officer in the Fort.

December came and the heat started again. Poor Father Antonio began to feel the return of his prickly heat, but it was not so severe this time as he had lost a lot of weight during the past nine months.

One lovely evening Joseph and Maria were again sitting in their favourite place watching the full moon rising over the sea. At first it was just a silvery mist in the blackness of the sky, and the stars shone down like a million brilliant diamonds; but as they watched, they saw the rim of the moon rise over the edge of the sea – blood red. It took form rapidly and in a few moments they saw it floating clear in the sky – a smoky golden ball, which, as it rose higher in the sky, gradually turned to bright silver and appeared to become smaller.

The light was so bright that Joseph could make out the blue of Maria's gown, and she could see the slashes of scarlet silk decorating the sleeves of his doublet. Below them, one of the soldiers was playing the guitar, plucking gently at the strings while some of the men sang softly. They sang some of the plaintive love songs of their native land. All was calm and beautiful.

Joseph turned to Maria and took her gently in his arms. Their lips met. "Marry me soon, my beloved," he pleaded with her. "I love you so much!"

He could see the moon reflected in her eyes, which shone with happiness as she whispered softly, "I love you too, Joseph, and I'll marry you as soon as you wish."

Hand in hand they went to seek Hadija's blessing, which was gladly given. "Your father will be happy," she said and kissed them affectionately. "Now off you go and look for Father Antonio. I think he's in the Chapel."

They found the Priest, who was delighted to hear of their betrothal.

"When can you marry us, Father?" Joseph asked.

"It's nearly Christmas, so I'll marry you on Christmas Eve, my children," the old man said smiling at them. They knelt as he blessed them. It was now only ten days until Christmas Eve and Joseph would have to be patient!

The period of peace for the island was coming to an end though, for three days later there was the cry of "Sails!" and the sails of a large fleet of ships were again seen in the north.

Everyone was hustled into the Fort once more, and the defences, which were always in a state of readiness, were checked to perfection. Then the defenders sat back to await developments ... these soon came!

They had not been the only ones to see the sails, and soon they could see crowds of Omani gathering near the Fort. The Commandant thought he would remind the enemy that the Fort still possessed teeth to bite with, and called Jose Barraso to him.

"Captain Barraso, I'm sure your men could do with some target practice! There are some very tempting targets just under the walls of the Fort whose health could be considerably improved by some exercise. Please provide them with the necessary exercise!"

Jose grinned at his Commandant and went off to give his orders and soon the enemy were effectively dispersed by musket fire, whilst a couple of grenades occasionally thrown in their direction kept them at a safe distance. The guards were doubled, for the Commandant wanted no repetition of the previous attack, while their attention was held by the oncoming ships.

As the vessels sailed closer, the people in the Fort could see that they were the enemy. Shots were exchanged as the five ships sailed into the channel leading to the harbour.

The defenders cheered as they saw a shot take effect. One of the ships heeled over and started to sink. Some of the men jumped off and swam, whilst others vanished beneath the water. The harbour was full of sharks which were always ready to seize an unwary swimmer. However, four out of the five ships sailed past the Fort defiantly, their drums beating, horns blowing and men chanting. The defenders of the Fort could hear the cheers as the Omani forces on the island welcomed the newcomers.

Soon reports came in from the spies. The enemy had been reinforced by seven hundred men from Muscat, of whom four hundred were African slaves.

That night flames rose high and shouts and screams rang out as this new army began to loot and pillage the old town of Mombasa. Kongowea and Mvita, where the majority of the Swahili people lived, and Gavana, the walled town near the Fort which was occupied mainly by the rich Arab and Portuguese merchants, were in flames. The people in the Fort watched with horror, unable to do anything to help these unfortunate people, as they were now outnumbered by the enemy.

"Why didn't they listen to our warnings and remain in the safety of the Fort?" the Commandant said despairingly to Father Antonio. He remembered that many of these people had returned to their homes of their own free will, in spite of warnings that the trouble was not yet over.

Late one night, soon after this, those in the Fort heard the drums thrumming out once again, accompanied by the usual shouts and blowing of war horns. They rushed to the ramparts and by straining their eyes into the darkness of the night, were able to make out a distant white gleam of sails in the starlight.

The guns of the Fort fired a couple of parting shots at the faintly-seen Omani ships, which, due to the darkness, managed to escape without injury. But all the time they kept up their defiant drumming and horn blowing until they were well out of range. It was heard afterwards that these ships had sailed for Muscat with a cargo of slaves taken from the old town after the raid.

As the days passed the atmosphere of the Fort grew tense once more. The heat pressed down upon them and quarrels broke out as passions rose. Father Antonio thought he would try and divert them by some means, so he gathered the women and children together – there were pitifully few by this time – and organised them into a group to decorate the Chapel for Christmas.

Christmas Eve dawned, and when the congregation went into the Chapel for the wedding of Joseph de Britto and Maria da Costa that morning, they gasped with amazement. The Chapel had been transformed by palm leaves and flowers, plucked outside the Fort and smuggled in by some means known only to the Priest. Father Antonio had even managed to find some candles and the building was a blaze of light!

Apart from the sentries, everyone in the Fort, whether Christian or Muslim, was in the Chapel for the wedding, for both the bride and groom were much loved and respected.

Joseph waited nervously at the steps of the altar, kneeling beside Jose Barraso. Very soon there was a flurry at the door and Joseph looked up to see Maria coming towards him on the arm of the Commandant. She wore her mother's wedding gown, and a white veil with a simple wreath of white flowers. She had never looked more beautiful!

With modestly downcast eyes and flushed cheeks, she reached Joseph's side, and after Father Antonio had conducted the ceremony and concluded the Nuptial Mass, they made their way out of the Chapel to the courtyard, where the cooks had managed to provide a feast for them all.

The atmosphere in the Fort was gay, and the day was made doubly happy by the fact that it was Christmas Eve. The Muslims, too, entered into the spirit of Christmas, for they had just finished the fast of Ramadhan and had sighted the new moon the previous night. The rejoicings carried on until midnight, when the Catholics filed into the Chapel for Mass.

Midnight Mass on this Christmas Eve was very moving, for the Chapel was still brightly lit by the many candles, and in spite of the danger which lay outside the walls of the Fort and the uncertainty of the future, there was peace in that sanctified place. The spicy clouds of incense rose in fragrant curls; voices rose and fell sweetly as the service proceeded in Latin. This Christmas Eve service was one which was remembered by those who took part for the rest of their lives.

After the end of the service, they left the Chapel silently and walked out into the soft, warm night. There was no snow in this country, but although their traditional atmosphere of snow and cold was missing, the Portuguese still felt very close to that first Christmas. The sky overhead was full of bright stars which seemed to glitter so closely, shining downwards from above the palm trees, that they almost felt they could touch them.

Chapter 18

The next morning, as the sun rose, the peace of the still sleeping Fort was shattered by the lookout's shoots of "Sails! Sails!"

Joseph, rushed, half-dressed, to the lookout tower and saw the sails of five large ships approaching from the south. They moved rapidly with a following wind, and soon a cheer arose as they were recognised as Portuguese warships.

"'Reinforcements at last!" Joseph shouted in delight. Then taking another look at the vessels, he ran to his quarters to finish dressing and eat a hasty breakfast before taking his place on the ramparts again.

The fleet was approaching the entrance to the harbour now, and danger lay in the fact that they were sailing into the harbour in broad daylight, as though the enemy did not exist.

"Oh, the stupid fools!" Joseph groaned, "Don't they realise that the Omani will be waiting for them, and will fight tooth and nail to prevent them from landing yet here they are sailing in as though they're on a fleet exercise!"

The vessels sailed boldly on into the harbour. They were a fine sight, with their white sails with the great red crosses billowing out in the wind and their pennants streaming from the tall masts. There was a flurry of activity as the men shortened sail and finally brought the ships skilfully to a point opposite the Fort and obeyed the order to anchor.

Joseph ran to the Commandant to warn him that the ships were preparing to land boats, and suggested that the soldiers in the Fort should be prepared to make a sortie to help them land, as they would almost certainly be ambushed by the Omani. The defenders in the Fort had no way of warning those on board of the strength of the enemy, and they feared the newcomers would walk straight into a trap.

Those watching from the Fort saw the first ship lower two small boats, which started to make for the shore. As they approached, they were fired on by the Omani who were lying concealed amongst the bushes.

The gate of the Fort was opened and Joseph put himself at the head of a strong party which had been hastily mustered.

"Come on, follow me!" he shouted urgently, gesturing them forward with his sword. "To the rescue! Our men are being ambushed!"

His men rushed out of the Fort and engaged the enemy in the rear so fiercely that soon they were forced to draw back, but not before they had caused much damage and many casualties. Indeed, only three out of the fifty men in the two boats reached the shore alive.

It did not take the men on the ships long to realise what was happening and they opened fire on the main Omani groups on the shore, causing havoc amongst the enemy. They were eventually forced by the fire from the ships and the fierce fighting of Joseph's men attacking their rear, to withdraw to a safe distance.

As soon as it was seen that everything was safe, more boats came ashore, and in one of them was the leader of the relief force, Admiral Luis Sampaio.

Joseph went down to the water's edge to meet the Admiral. He had a tall thin figure, with sandy hair going thin on the top and grey around the temples. He had the sallow complexion of the chronic sufferer from dyspepsia, and a few moments conversation told Joseph that he was dealing with a weak, indecisive man.

"Is this the usual reception offered to His Majesty's fleet, Sir?" he asked Joseph plaintively. "I do not care for our welcome!"

Joseph, being a junior officer, kept a discreet silence. It was not for him to inform the Admiral that the debacle had been due to his lack of foresight and stupidity.

Luis Sampaio was still quivering from the reception his fleet had been given, so leaving his officers to see to the off-loading of men and stores, and the setting of guards, he asked Joseph to escort him to the Commandant of the Fort in order to pay his formal respects.

They walked through the Fort and stopped before the Commandant's door. Joseph knocked.

"Come in!" came the reply in gruff tones.

The Commandant looked up from his desk as they hesitated in the door. "Come in, come in!" he said sharply again, with a frown on his face.

"The Admiral, Sir," said Joseph respectfully. He could appreciate the feelings of the Commandant, for he too was angry at the incompetence and useless loss of life.

The Commandant rose to greet his visitor, whom he knew slightly, having met him in Goa several years before. His opinion of Luis Sampaio had not been very high even in those early days, and after the abortive landing of the morning, his opinion of the man had sunk even lower. His eyes were scornful as he took in his visitor's white face and trembling limbs. He controlled his temper, however, and greeted the Admiral with the courtesy his rank demanded.

"We are glad to see your fleet, Admiral," he said and pulling forward a chair for his guest, he called for wine.

"We have been very hard-pressed by the enemy and have suffered heavy losses from disease over the past few months; the extra men and supplies you bring will enable us to hold out a little longer. I have no doubt that you will report our dangerous situation to the authorities upon your return to Goa!"

The wine arrived and the Commandant gestured the other two men to go into the next room, where there were chairs set around a table. These chairs, which he had brought over from

Goa with him, were of carved ebony, inlaid with ivory chips; the backs and seats were of wicker.

The three men sat down and the Commandant poured out the wine. "Your health, Sir!" he bowed to the Admiral, who took the goblet in his trembling hands and drank deeply. The Commandant poured him more wine and when the Admiral had recovered from his shock, the three men had a serious discussion about their position.

"We will remain in Mombasa for a month," the Admiral said eventually in reply to a question. "Then we'll sail on to Goa."

Luis Sampaio told them that he had brought them fresh supplies and five hundred men to swell the garrison. There were cases of badly needed arms and ammunition; barrels of gunpowder and shot, and the courtyard of the Fort was a hive of feverish activity. Men were moving rapidly here and there; stowing stores, piling arms in the armoury, and the powder, and shot in the gunpowder store.

Old and new friends were meeting and greeting each other. The new arrivals were noticable, for they were still fair-skinned and red with sunburn, whereas many of the old-timers at the Fort were burnt almost black. On the whole, the new arrivals were much fitter and fatter than the defendants, who had lost any spare flesh over the past few months of short rations and fever, and were now mainly muscle and sinew. Even Father Antonio had lost weight and was slim, brown, and active, looking years younger in spite of the grey sprinkled in his thick hair and beard.

The Admiral told them that his fleet had sailed from Portugal, then after calling in at Goa, had gone straight to Mozambique, where they had been informed of the siege. There they had loaded additional stores and men and had sailed up to Mombasa to the rescue as fast as possible.

There was great rejoicing in the Fort that night and talking went on until early morning.

"We thought we'd been forgotten!" the Commandant remarked to the Admiral. "Your arrival has certainly raised the morale of my men!"

Life in the Fort was easy for the next month. The new men settled down and it was not long before they were looking as sunburnt as those who had been in the Fort for many months.

During this period the enemy kept very quiet, apart from one attempt to board the ships, which was foiled when one of the look-outs on board spotted some men trying to climb up the anchor chains. He had heard a faint splash in the sea and, thinking it must have been a fish, strolled curiously to the side of the ship. He glanced over and saw several heads bobbing about in the water. The Omani were trying to attack the ships! The swimming men were naked and covered with grease; they held their knives in their teeth as they swam along noiselessly towards the ships. Their intention had evidently been to creep up the anchor chains and attack the crew by stealth.

"To arms! To arms! The enemy are boarding!" The warning cry rang through the fleet.

Men rushed to the sides of the ships and immediately the swimmers were the targets for javelins, rocks and other missiles. Musket men were soon in position and aimed their weapons into the water at the attackers. In no time the water was clear of swimmers – only one or two corpses floating out on the tide.

The enemy kept away from the ships after that!

With the extra men, Joseph was able to organise sorties which cleared a safe area for half a mile around the Fort. This gave confidence to the local Swahilis, and supplies of fresh food were now being brought in regularly. The Commandant did not neglect the opportunity to keep the Fort fully stocked against any emergency and made the most of the lull in hostilities.

One day Joseph decided to take the war to the enemy camp. Calling for twenty volunteers, he proposed they should recapture the small Fort Joseph from the Omani. This idea was greeted with enthusiasm, and it was with suppressed excitement that they started out one night.

Joseph and his volunteers let themselves quietly into the tunnel. It was dark and the damp walls shone in the gleam of their dim lanterns. Before long they felt a cool breeze on their faces and knew they were near the end of the tunnel. Joseph ordered the lanterns to be put out and they groped their way carefully forward in the dark. As they drew near the entrance, they could see by the faint glimmer of moonlight that they had reached the entrance of a cave which overlooked the rear of Fort Joseph.

Creeping cautiously forward, Joseph saw the head of a sentry just below him, facing the sea. Moving swiftly and silently, he put his hand suddenly around the man's mouth, plunging his dagger into the body before he had a chance to raise the alarm. Joseph then whispered to the rest of the party to move forward and soon they were inside the walls of the little fort. Ahead of them in the stone building they could see a light and heard voices in loud conversation.

"Follow me," whispered Joseph and crawling up to the building, he peered in at the small opening which served as a window.

There were several Omani seated about a low table and it was obviously their meal time. Great bowls of rice and meat were on the table and the men, who had removed their weapons for comfort, were all dipping their hands into the communal bowls and gulping down the food at a great rate. Any thought of danger was far from their minds.

"We must rush them," Joseph whispered. "Take them by surprise and don't give them a chance to reach for their weapons!"

The door of the building stood wide open – the men inside obviously felt secure from attack and were suffering from the heat. Joseph gave the signal and his twenty armed men rushed into the room. The surprise was certainly complete!

There was almost no resistance and in a short time Fort Joseph was once more in their hands. Joseph then arranged to garrison the little Fort, for he intended using it as a forward base for attacks against the Omani.

Chapter 19

It was with a sense of shock that they realised one day that the time had at last come for the fleet to set sail again. The Commandant's only consolation was that when the ships sailed, they would take the dyspeptic Luis with them.

Luis Sampaio had regained his composure, but still suffered from indigestion and the heat, and his temper was uncertain in consequence. He spent most of the month in the Fort complaining about trivialities, and because of this he was not popular. His brother officers tolerated him only because they had no option, little realising that he was really shy and nervous.

Jose Barraso was to leave with the ships and was sad at parting from his companions. He had matured since his trip to Mozambique, and was now self-assured and very popular both with his men and his fellow officers. Before he left, he walked all round the fortress saying goodbye to the men. Hassani had pleaded to be allowed to accompany him, and the Commandant had given his permission, much to his delight. Jose didn't want to leave the men with whom he had shared so much danger, but Antonio Mogo de Mello had insisted that Jose should go to give the Governor in Goa a true picture of what had happened in Mombasa. He was also to give his opinions as to what was likely to happen in the near future and to plead for more reinforcements if the Fort was to be kept from falling into enemy hands.

The Commandant had no illusions about Luis Sampaio; he realised that he lacked the courage to stand up and plead with the Governor for the men and supplies needed to win the siege of Fort Jesus. The Commandant knew also that with all the trouble at present in Europe, the Governor would be reluctant to send ships and men he could ill spare to a small place like Mombasa. So unless Jose persuaded the Governor that it was urgent to send reinforcements, they would have to depend on their own slender resources to hold the Fort.

Finally, Jose went to the Officers' quarters to say goodbye to the Commandant. He put his arm affectionately around Jose's shoulder, for he was fond of the young man, and gruffly wished him 'Godspeed'.

"We'll all miss you, Captain Barraso!" he said sadly. Jose had tears in his eyes.

"I hate to go, Sir," he said with emotion. "I'm leaving all my best friends here!"

Jose's thoughts went back to that night before he made the journey which was to make him rise to manhood; many faces had changed since then, and he wondered with sadness how many of his friends he would meet again. He pulled himself together and stood stiffly to attention, for first and foremost he was a soldier! He saluted his Commandant smartly and marched through the door.

Joseph joined him and accompanied him until they were outside the massive gates of the Fort. They walked silently, each wrapped in his own thoughts. At the water's edge, Jose turned and gazed for a long time at the towering fortress above him, as though he wished to engrave it upon his memory for ever. He felt that he would never see it again, but it still claimed all his love and allegiance.

He sighed deeply, turned round and held his hand out to Joseph. "May God be with you, Sir," he said with emotion.

Then he stepped quickly into the small boat where the seamen were waiting to take him to the flagship. Luis was already seated in the boat, and with a last wave, they set off. Joseph returned sadly to the Fort.

They sailed on the outgoing tide that afternoon, and apart from the essential look-outs, the whole garrison lined the ramparts to watch the huge sails billow out as they filled with wind. The five great ships of the squadron sailed slowly out of the harbour and set off east towards Goa.

The people in the Fort watched until all trace of the ships had vanished, then they turned sadly aside, feeling suddenly lonely, for they realised they were on their own again.

Chapter 20

A year had passed since the siege had begun. There had been many changes and deaths since that time, and now they were in middle of the hot season again. Every evening clouds came up on the horizon, only to disappear again. It grew hotter and more humid as the days went by.

The enemy, who had been keeping quiet for several weeks, grew bolder after the departure of the ships and made several attempts to attack the Fort; but each time they were repulsed with heavy losses. The rains came at last at the end of March, but the cooler weather also brought a plague of mosquitoes, and fever was rife throughout the garrison.

It had not been possible to guard the large area that had been freed from the enemy, now that there were fewer men, and they had to be constantly on watch if they went outside the perimeter of the Fort. After three of their men had been attacked while on a foray to obtain fresh fruit and vegetables, Joseph and the Commandant decided that discipline would have to be tightened. No one was allowed to leave the Fort without a pass, even when they went on duty to Fort Joseph. This garrison was still being maintained, but the Commandant was seriously considering withdrawing his men in view of the changing situation. In the meantime, the rule about passes was very strictly enforced and the slightest infringement was heavily punished. There was, naturally, a lot of grumbling about this order for a lot of the men had women in the town they used to visit, but the rule had been made in the interests of the safety of the Fort as a whole, and not for the convenience of a few malcontents.

At this time a curious thing happened. A woman, who was heavily veiled, came to the gate saying she wished to speak to Leonardo Nunes. He was called and they spoke together in a corner out of earshot of the gate guards. Then the woman left. That night, when Leonardo was to go on sentry duty, it was found that he was missing from his bed. A search was made throughout the Fort but no trace of him was found. Then it was discovered that his weapons had disappeared as well as some of his personal belongings, and it was presumed that he had deserted and left the Fort with a forged pass. This was confirmed when Joseph found that the sentry guarding the gate had passed through the relief guard for Fort Joseph, and that Leonardo Nunes had been amongst them. They were, however, destined to see him again.

Soon after this incident, one of the soldiers was walking across the courtyard on his way to his quarters. A few people were idly watching him and were surprised when he staggered and fell heavily. They rushed over and picked him up and took him along to the doctor.

At first the doctor thought he had heat stroke, and bent down to have a closer look at him, at the same time undoing the man's garments. When he straightened up again after his examination, his face was very grave.

"Keep this man completely isolated," he said to the woman who was assisting him. "No one is to come near him!"

He called to Father Antonio, who had been hurrying across to see what the trouble was. "Father! I'm going to see the Commandant. Will you come with me?"

The Priest joined him and together they walked swiftly to the Commandant's quarters. "Come in!" he called out in answer to their knock. He looked surprised to see the doctor and the

Priest standing together on the threshold. However, he invited them to sit down.

"I'm afraid I've very grave news for you, Sir," said the doctor. He was very pale and spoke hurriedly.

"What is it, Doctor?" asked the Commandant.

"Our worst misfortune yet, I'm afraid!" replied the doctor. "I've just attended to a very sick man, and I fear he has the Black Plague!"

"Black Plague!" gasped the Commandant with fear in his voice. "May God help us all and have mercy upon our souls!"

The three men looked at each other in horror and crossed themselves.

"I'm sure of it, Sir, for I saw cases in Italy, Spain and Portugal when the plague was raging there. I don't know how long this man was moving about amongst his comrades before he collapsed, but I'm afraid his won't be the only case."

Quick action had to be taken! The Commandant issued immediate orders that anyone who felt or looked ill must immediately be isolated from the others. Once again part of the Fort was set aside as a hospital and volunteers came forward to help with the nursing. These volunteers were men and women who had already suffered from the plague and recovered, and were therefore immune to further attacks. That night there were three fresh cases, and the first man died before morning. The Commandant ordered that his body be burnt to try and prevent the plague from spreading. The clothing of those who fell ill was also immediately burnt, but in spite of these precautions, nothing could stop the plague from spreading.

Now began a period of horror in the Fort, for as the weeks passed, more people died; the plague attacked them swiftly and usually fatally. Soon there were very few people left who had not succumbed.

Even the women did double guard duty, and it was as well that they took greater precautions, for one night they were again attacked and the enemy nearly succeeded in forcing their way into the Fort. However, the defendants fought them off with great bravery, without the enemy ever realising how depleted their forces were.

The Commandant, Joseph and Father Antonio seemed to be everywhere at once, their swords flashing. It was only after the enemy had been repulsed with heavy losses, that the Commandant staggered and fell. When Joseph and the doctor reached him, they found that he had a gaping hole in his right side. They hastily called some men, who carefully carried the wounded man to his quarters, where he was nursed devotedly by Maria and her mother. He grew feverish, and at one time was so delirious he had to be held down. But at last, thanks to the women's care, he slowly began to recover, although, for a long time, he was very weak and ill.

Chapter 21

The situation in the Fort was by now very serious. The plague continued to claim victims, and by the end of June only a handful of Portuguese, a few Arabs and Swahilis had survived; there were not more than two hundred and fifty people in all. There was a shortage of men to keep guard, so some of the women dressed as men and walked the ramparts as sentries, so that the enemy could have no idea of the grim reality within the walls of the Fort. The ruse worked, for the Fort was not attacked again.

They needed all their courage to face this terrible time. Eventually the remaining officers consulted together and it was decided that one of their number would have to go for help. Joseph was chosen, for he was the fittest and would be able to command respect and get a hearing from the Governor of Mozambique.

They had learned a lot from the journey of Jose Barraso, and this time Joseph was going with just one other companion. Miguel, who had had the plague, but recovered, was chosen to accompany him. He had done the journey before and would be able to help and advise him, as he was familiar with the coast all the way to Mozambique.

Joseph decided they should disguise themselves as Swahili traders, as in this way they would have more chance of getting through the enemy held territory, especially as the Omani now held Zanzibar.

When all their plans were complete and they were ready to depart, Joseph went with Maria to Father Antonio. "I ask your blessing, Father," he said, and they both knelt before him.

"You have my blessing, my son," said the old man. "May God go with you and give you a safe journey."

"Father, I leave my wife in your care. Guard her well, for she is my most cherished possession," begged Joseph.

"I'll guard her with my prayers and my life!" promised the Priest, and blessed the couple. He left them kneeling together in the Chapel, praying for strength to endure the sorrowful parting.

After Maria and Joseph left the Chapel, they took a turn on the ramparts before going to their quarters. They did not talk much, as their hearts were too full for words. But when they reached their favourite sheltered place, Joseph took his wife tenderly in his arms; only then did she break down and weep bitterly. It was the one time she cried over their parting and she soon had control over her emotions. They stood looking over the old Fort, so strong and protective, and thought back over their short married life. Somehow they had faith that this parting was for a short time only, and Maria had a sudden calm conviction that Joseph would come back to her safely.

All too soon their few precious hours together passed, and as there were still a lot of preparations to be made, they made their way with reluctance to their quarters. Joseph went to see the Commandant, while Maria prepared a meal.

She knew her husband must eat well before he set out on his journey, although she had no stomach for cookery or eating. However, by the time he returned, she had a tasty meal waiting on the table. They ate in silence, watching each other with sadness in their eyes. Then they went to bed. Joseph had to rise at 4 a.m. to start on his long journey before daybreak, in order to get well clear of Mombasa before the sun rose.

They lay in each other's arms, trying to find what comfort they could. All too soon there was a knock, on the door, and Joseph had to get up and say goodbye to his wife. She lay tearless; although her eyes were large and dark in her pale face. He kissed her for the last time before he joined Miguel, who was waiting outside the door.

"Goodbye, my darling," she whispered. "May God take care of your!"

"May He protect you, my Maria," answered Joseph, and he went on his way.

Very quietly the two men slipped out of the small gate to their boat. All was silent, and when dawn rose they were well on their way to Mozambique.

Chapter 22

Three weeks after Joseph's departure, Maria was walking slowly along the ramparts with her mother. Although it was early morning, she was very pale and, even as Hadija looked at her, she swayed and nearly fell.

"Maria! Whatever's the matter?" Hadija asked her in a worried voice.

"I feel so ill, Mother!" Maria whispered faintly. Putting her arm around her daughter, Hadija helped her to their quarters and made her lie down.

"Quick! a bowl, Mother, I want to be sick!"

Maria vomited and to her mother's dismay a green froth appeared on her lips. Hadija started to undress her. Maria's skin was burning and she lay back on the pillow, almost unconscious. Her mother removed her bodice, and as she did so she started back in horror, gazing at the livid pustule which had formed in Maria's armpit.

"Oh, God help you, my daughter! It's the plague!" Hadija sank to her knees beside the bed and wept bitterly.

However, she was a brave woman and soon pulled herself together, for being an experienced nurse, she knew that there was no time to be lost. Wrapping Maria in clean clothes, she went for Father Antonio, who hurried back with her to Maria's bedside and remained there praying. He shared the work of watching over her and bathing her body with cool water, taking turns with Hadija to rest.

Maria's temperature rose, and by evening she was tossing and turning in delirium, her skin hot and dry and her voice husky. The pustule had swollen rapidly and the skin was stretched tight and shining over it, so that she cried out in agony at the slightest touch.

The doctor had called in earlier to see her and told Hadija gravely, "If she can survive tonight, and if the pustule bursts and releases its poison, then she has a faint chance of recovering. It's touch and go now!"

They worked on trying to bring her temperature down by wrapping her in cold, wet clothes, which they renewed constantly. At length Maria lay still and white, with her eyes closed.

Hadija broke down at last. "Maria, Maria, don't leave me!" she cried. Father Antonio put a comforting arm around her heaving shoulders.

At that moment Maria gave a piercing scream and half sat up in the bed, then fell back unconscious again. Her mother and the Priest rushed to her side and saw she had broken out into a sweat. Hadija raised the sheet which covered her and looked. "God be praised, the pustule has burst!" she sobbed. "Now we can save her!"

Feverishly they worked on Maria again, and by morning, although they were almost dropping with strain and weariness, their faces shone with joy. They knew for certain now that with careful nursing Maria would live! She had opened her eyes, and recognising the anxious faces bending over her, had given them a weak smile. She had passed safely through the 'Valley of Shadows', thanks to the devoted nursing of her mother and Father Antonio. Now, although still very ill, she was out of danger.

She made a slow recovery and it was a couple of weeks before Hadija allowed her out of bed. Gradually her strength returned, and ten days later she was able to walk very slowly on the ramparts, holding Hadija's arm. The cool breeze from the sea blew around them, catching at their gowns as they walked towards the chair that had been placed in the shade for Maria.

"I wonder how Joseph is faring?" she murmured to Hadija. "It seems so long since he left Mombasa, and so much has happened during the past few weeks!"

"My dear, I know exactly how you feel," her mother replied. "For I miss my husband, your dear father, more every day."

"Have you had news of him lately, Mother?" asked Maria.

"He wrote to say he had been recalled to Portugal," Hadija replied. "But he expected to be able to return to Goa by the end of the year and he wants me to try and join him there on his return. He thinks we're safe here. He's heard nothing of the siege, as he left Goa several months ago as you know."

"News travels so slowly," said Maria thoughtfully. "I wish there were some way of sending it quickly through the air!"

"We can only send our loving thoughts and prayers winging through the air in hope," replied her mother with a sigh.

Chapter 23

The atmosphere was hot, and the slight breeze smelt of the promised rain. All along the horizon to the south and south-east the sky was a threatening steel-grey stormy colour toning to paler grey at the edges; in front of this menacing picture, rode heavy clumps of snow-white clouds, pushed into fanciful shapes by the rising wind.

Walking on the ramparts, Maria looked at the storm which was rapidly riding towards the island, borne on the wings of the south wind. Her thoughts were, as usual, of her husband, and she prayed constantly for his safety. In her imagination she could see the small boat being tossed on the crest of the white-topped waves. It was a long weary journey he had to take, and a very perilous one.

Maria was regaining her strength rapidly, but looked sad as she worried about her young husband. Joseph had been gone nearly two months now. At last there seemed to have been a lull in the plague, but those in the Fort were weary, dispirited and many were ill with various fevers.

Maria's thoughts turned to the Commandant, who was slowly dying from his wound which had become gangrenous; there was no known treatment, apart from constant fresh dressings.

They had kept him alive so far by careful nursing, but he was very near the end now. Hadija was nursing him most of the time, but Father Antonio would relieve her every few hours so that she could snatch a few hours rest and fresh air. Maria would also take a turn in the sick room which was foul with the stench of the Commandant's putrifying wound; none of them could stand it for very long.

Mogo de Mello was hollow-cheeked and his skin had taken on the look of grey parchment they had seen so often on the faces of the dying. Father Antonio was with him and had administered the last rites, and now it was only the Commandant's own great will-power which kept him alive.

He was a brave man and they would miss him. Even at this stage he was conscious, but suffered quietly and without complaint. Surely Maria thought, it would have been more fitting for this soldier, with the instincts of a monk, to have been killed outright in battle, instead of rotting to death in this slow degrading way!

Again Maria's mind turned to her husband; she supposed it would be many weary weeks before they were together again. She refused to doubt that this day would come.

The wind increased over the fortress and blew the hair streaming back from her face as she looked out towards the sea. It was nearly black as the sky darkened with the coming storm, and she could see the rain sweeping in like a heavy grey curtain.

The sea below the Fort was a dark grey swirling mass of water, topped by choppy little waves with curling white tops. As the tide was in, it crashed against the coral cliffs at the base of the Fort, throwing itself high against the land with sullen fury and flying spray.

The first few drops of rain splashed down; the heat and humidity seemed to become even more oppressive, and Maria could smell the wet dust where the rain had fallen. There was a curious stillness in the air – a sense of waiting – and beyond the walls of the Fort, somewhere in the old town, a dog howled a long quivering note. Maria shuddered and crossed herself.

Soon, however, the curtain of rain fell heavily and she had to run for shelter from the heavy, stinging drops. As she stood under the ramparts the rain splashed and streamed down as though poured from a gigantic bucket. She could hear the hissing and splashing as it fell, filling the courtyard with mud and water.

The sentries huddled in their covered shelters and those who had urgent messages to deliver made frantic dashes through the rain, arriving at their destinations soaked through. The rest of the people huddled together miserably like wet chickens, wincing every time there was a flash of lightning and a roll of thunder.

Maria made her way back to Mogo de Mello's room, and was met at the door by Father Antonio, who was on his way to find her.

"It's finished, my child!" he said with a sigh. "A fine man has gone. God rest his soul!"

Maria crossed herself and felt very sad, for she had admired the Moor. Death, however, was no respecter of persons and his finger pointed at high and low, good and bad alike.

Antonio Mogo de Mello's death meant that her cousin, Prince Daud of Faza, would have to assume command of the Fort and its defences.

Maria went to the Chapel with Father Antonio to pray for the soul of the Commandant, and for the protection and safety of those remaining in the Fort.

The storm subsided as suddenly as it had arisen, and as the evening dusk deepened, stars could be seen faintly sparkling in the sky above. There was a refreshing smell of fresh wet earth and leaves wafting on the breeze, and a faint smell of wood cooking-fires.

For the moment the Fort was impregnable and at peace. Death, disease and destruction came, but still it remained, towering and strong, as though daring mere man to overcome it.

Chapter 24

Early one morning, as August faded into September, there was a loud shout from one of the lookouts that there were ships on the horizon. He shouted with excitement that there were two groups of sails to be seen in the early morning haze. One group was approaching from the south and the other from the north!

There was a flurry and rush and the ramparts facing seaward were soon crowded as everyone left in the Fort rushed to see the oncoming ships. As the two fleets sailed closer, the watchers could make out through their spy-glasses that the ones from the south were Portuguese warships, and the ones from the north were the familiar fighting ships of the Omani. Fate had decreed that they should arrive outside Mombasa at the same time!

Breathlessly, those in the Fort watched as the two fleets, battle pennants flying, drew nearer together, until at last they came within firing distance, just outside the entrance to the harbour. Puffs of smoke rose out of the sides of the vessels and they could hear the sound of cannonfire, which seemed to rumble over the sea towards them.

Suddenly there was a shout as the mast of one of the Omani ships shattered and fell. They could see men who had been swept into the sea by falling canvas, desperately trying to climb the shrouds and rigging in an attempt to climb on board again and escape from drowning.

Another of the five Omani ships burst into flames, which roared through its rigging. The watchers saw a couple of small boats put out from the stricken vessel, and the men in them rowing frenziedly away from the burning vessel. Other men were seen flinging themselves overboard in an effort to escape the flames. Then there was a dull 'boom' and more flames and smoke rose up in a column as the ammunition on the ship blew up. The blast threw the frail boats out of the water and heads could be seen bobbing about in the sea; then the stricken ship rolled over and sank rapidly. When the smoke cleared, the heads and ship had disappeared from sight.

There were more shouts from the watchers in the Fort as one of the five Portuguese ships drew alongside and grappled with an Omani vessel. Swarms of men jumped onto the deck of the enemy ship and fierce fighting broke out.

Carlos and Hussein were beside themselves with excitement as they could see groups of men fighting all over the decks. Eventually, after putting up fierce resistance, the enemy ship was captured, and towed into Mombasa as a prize.

By this time the Omani had had enough of the fight and the watchers saw, through the smoke and haze of the battle, their two remaining ships turn away and sail back north, hotly pursued by shots from the victors.

There were loud cheers from the Fort when this happened. "They're beaten!" yelled Carlos to Hussein, and the two boys jumped up and down with excitement.

The five victorious Portuguese ships then turned and made their way gracefully into the harbour, towing their captive vessel behind them.

However, they were not to be permitted to land so easily, for they found themselves fired on by the angry and disappointed Omani troops who had been left on the island, and had seen their fleet defeated.

The ships returned the fire, but a shot from the shore damaged the steering gear of one of them. It swung round out of control, and to the horror of the watchers in the Fort, and amid cheers from the jubilant Omani, it was swept by the current and wind towards the rocks. All was not lost, however, for one of the other vessels, seeing its plight, sailed close and their men threw out ropes. They were joined by another ship and eventually between them they succeeded in pulling the stricken vessel clear of the rocks and helped it to anchor just off the shore below the Fort.

The guns on the ships had by this time been turned towards the Omani on the shore and soon those on board considered it safe enough to attempt to land a boat from the damaged vessel. Those in the Fort could see three boats being launched which, after rowing hard, managed to make their way against the current into smoother water. They pitched up at the foot of the Fort.

A party from the Fort now decided to sally forth to help the newcomers; Prince Daud and Father Antonio led the pitifully small party through the gates.

By this time the ships were launching landing parties. However, the men from the Fort crept quietly down the cliff path where, on rounding a corner, they came up against a group of Omani troops hiding in the bushes ready to ambush the men from the ships. With great courage the men from the Fort attacked, and immediately the air was filled with the clash of weapons, and the groans and cries of fighting men.

Troops from the ship landed and with fierce war-cries went to the rescue of the small but gallant party. The enemy broke under their fierce onslaught and scattered, aiming a few last sword thrusts as they went. It was one of these that pierced the lung of Father Antonio. He fell to the ground, bright red blood staining his robe, just as Joseph de Britto fought his way to his side.

"Father! Father!" shouted the young man and, running across to him, took the wounded priest in his arms.

"Joseph, my good friend," gasped the Priest faintly, "thank God you're back. You're just in time to save the Fort. Your Maria is well and waiting for you."

"We must carry you up to the Fort, Father," said Joseph in despair.

"No, leave me here my son, it's a fatal wound." He paused for breath. "Listen to me, for I've only a short time... I promised Carlos' father that I would care for him... will you.. take on.. that charge for me?"

"Yes, Father," said Joseph with tears in his eyes. "Carlos will be brought up as my own son."

The Priest eyes were growing dim, but he smiled at Joseph. "God bless... you... for that promise... Joseph!" His voice grew fainter and the light faded from his eyes as he died. Joseph put his hands over his face and wept like a child, for he had loved Father Antonio dearly.

Sorrowfully the men carried the body back to the Fort, where it was received with much weeping and wailing. Father Antonio had been loved by all for his big, generous heart. He was mourned by Christians and Muslims alike. Joseph's arrival was saddened by the tragedy. He walked through the gate of the Fort with his head bowed in grief.

"Joseph! Oh, Joseph!" there was a sudden cry, and with a sob Maria flung herself into his arms.

"You're here! You're safe!" Maria sobbed, leaning against his shoulder.

"Thank God you're safe, Maria my love," he said and tears came into his eyes again as he looked at his wife and saw how thin she had grown during his absence.

The Commander of the troops, who was their old colleague, Luis Sampaio, came up to them. There were more shocks for Joseph, when he learned to his horror and grief, that little Carlos was the only surviving Portuguese male in the Fort. Plague, malaria, dysentery, fever and wounds had decimated all the others.

At last Joseph was able to bring order out of chaos, and after a few hours of hard work, he was able to snatch an hour alone with Maria. He had been very distressed when Hadija told him how very nearly he had lost his wife. He now sat holding her hand.

"What was your journey like?" Maria asked him.

"Very long and tiring, but uneventful," he replied. "We saw plenty of porpoises and flying fish. The heat was the worst part of it and we were very nearly capsized by a curious whale. However, we were lucky, the wind blew continuously from the north so that we were able to make rapid progress and sail straight to Mozambique without having to put ashore anywhere on the way. Our only stop was at the first village Jose Barraso had told us about, where we were given a great welcome. Our water was finished towards the end of the journey but we were saved after two days thirst by a sudden heavy squall of rain. We were able to catch enough water for the remaining three days that it took us to reach Mozambique.

"When we sailed into the harbour, we found to our joy that a fleet had just arrived from Goa and so we were able to set sail almost immediately to relieve Fort Jesus. We were almost too late it seems!"

In spite of losing her old friend, Hadija was happier than she had been for a long time, for she had received a letter from her husband, which had been forwarded from Portugal. It had been written a couple of months before, but she now felt she was in touch with him.

Prince Daud was happy to hand over his responsibility as Commandant to Luis Sampaio, and soon the Fort was once again the scene of great activity as boats shuttled to and fro from the ships and the shore, landing men and supplies.

There were three hundred new troops and a good pile of stores and provisions. Another doctor also arrived, which was a great relief, as the Fort's only doctor had died of plague several weeks earlier. There was both sadness and joy in the hearts of those in the Fort that night. They grieved for their friend, Father Antonio, and they knew he would have been the first one to have rejoiced with them at Joseph's safe return. Now that the Fort was quieter, they all missed him, particularly the two young boys, Carlos and Hussein, who had looked on him as their father.

A few mornings later they watched the fleet sailing out with the tide. The fifth ship had been pulled off the reef at high tide by the others, the steering gear had been repaired and now all five vessels were on their way to Goa.

"I'll do my best to make them listen to me in Goa, and send a large expedition to retake the whole island and garrison the Fort properly," Commander Pereira da Silva told them before he left. "Those in authority don't understand the situation and underestimate the power of the Omani."

"They've the crazy idea that we can hold out for years without any further assistance," replied Joseph bitterly. "Just look at the waste of life already! We have to run to Mozambique for help every time we're attacked, and each time we have fewer soldiers left to defend the Fort. One day it'll be too late, and Portugal will lose Mombasa simply because they're more interested in the affairs of Europe!"

"Cheer up, my friend, all is not yet lost!" said Commander da Silva cheerfully as he turned to go. "I'll see you in a few weeks time, for we're due to load more stores and troops for Mozambique and should be back here just after Christmas. Who knows, the Government in Goa may relent and give me more troops and guns for you."

With a cheery wave, he went aboard his flagship.

One afternoon about ten days after the fleet had left, Luis Sampaio complained of a violent headache. He was soon shivering, and at the same time burned with a raging fever. He lost consciousness, and to everyone's horror, died in a fit of convulsions before morning. It was the dreaded 'Brain Fever' which often attacked newcomers to Africa.

Luis had been thought to be a coward, but in the end Joseph had come to admire him. He realised that he was a kindly man, more suited to the life of a scholar than that of a soldier; he was tortured by indigestion, which was the result of his nervous disposition. "Perhaps Luis was braver than a lot of other men!" Joseph thought to himself.

This sudden death meant that Joseph was now the Commandant of the Fort, and the first thing he did was to call a meeting of all his officers and plan a completely new defence system. His wisdom in making this move was proved only too well about two weeks later. One evening the alarm was given and the men heard the familiar drums beating. They promptly fired in the direction of the sound, for being a black night, they were unable to see their enemy. But in the morning spies came to tell them that four Omani ships had sailed unscathed into the harbour under the cover of darkness, and even now were unloading men and supplies.

In spite of the fresh enemy troops, the defenders of the Fort were still in command of the situation, beating off a few minor attacks which were half-heartedly launched by the Omani.

They even carried on a little trading with the Nyika people, who used to bring them fresh supplies in exchange for cloth and other goods. These traders would paddle over from the mainland in their canoes and land at the bottom of the Fort, where men would be sent out to trade with them.

Life continued this way for a few weeks, with both sides wary of starting a major offensive.

Chapter 25

Only the presence of the Omani ships in the distance reminded the defenders of the Fort that there was still need for vigilance. Soon, however, the enemy ships also sailed away and peace reigned once more for a while.

One of the new officers to have been landed off the Portuguese ships was Captain Jacome de Morais. He was brave and reckless, and the two boys, Carlos and Hussein, hung around him like a couple of puppies. He was a big, broad man, with a great red beard, a deep laugh and a healthy appetite for wine, women, song and danger.

Indeed, danger and Jacome de Morais were old acquaintances, so much so that he would wear a bright red coat when he walked on the ramparts in the daytime, and a white coat at night for, he said, "It will help the poor devils to pick me out!"

He was often shot at, but he seemed to bear a charmed life and merely laughed at the danger. It was Jacome who took Carlos and Hussein in hand and taught them to fight. "Like men, not like milk-sops!" When they grew up they were both renowned fighters, for Jacome was one of the finest swordsmen in Portugal. Every spare moment he had during the next few weeks he could be found giving the boys lessons in swordsmanship and wrestling.

One evening there was a great commotion in the town at the foot of the Fort. Women and children were screaming, men shouting and here and there fires were seen blazing. Joseph immediately doubled the guard and sent out a spy to find out what was causing the commotion. He learned that the Omani had decided to raid the town, as they believed the townsfolk were helping the defenders of the Fort.

They showed no mercy and had even enlisted the aid of the Musungulos, who were, at this period, angry with the Portuguese, whom they considered had been withholding trade goods from them without reason.

The people in the Fort were heavily outnumbered, and dared not go out to attempt a rescue. They could only listen with horror to the commotion and the heart-rending screams which went on till well towards dawn; then the fires died down and a heavy silence fell over the town.

Apart from the knowledge that the townspeople had been attacked, they had no further news until three days later when a ragged, filthy figure of a man, leading an equally ragged, filthy woman staggered up to the gate and implored to be allowed in – it was Leonardo Nunes the deserter! But what a change! He had become a shattered wreck of a man; wild-eyed and on the verge of a mental breakdown.

His story was a pitiful one, and his only thought was to avenge himself on the Omanis. He told Joseph that he had become a deserter for love of his wife and child. He had accepted the Muslim faith when he had had a child by her. This child was the idol of his life and it was because he could not bear to be separated from his family that he had left the Fort when his wife had come to tell him that the child was very ill. The child had recovered, and Leonardo Nunes, knowing that death was the penalty for desertion had stayed with them, living very quietly in their little hut on the outskirts of the old town.

One evening, a few days before, he had heard a slight sound, and looking up from the work he was doing, had gazed straight into the cruel eyes of an Omani! He jumped up and seized the man by the throat, but soon more and more of the enemy arrived and he fell under a rain of blows, and was knocked and kicked unconscious.

When at last he came to his senses, he found he had been tied to a tree and that there was a band of Omani sitting near him eating. He tried to move, and found that the ropes holding his wrists were fairly slack. He writhed and twisted about, and pulled and rubbed at his bonds, but somehow could not free himself. In the meantime darkness had fallen and the Omani had lit great fires. He could hear cries and shouts for help coming from the town and saw the glare of great flames leaping high into the air.

All at once there was a commotion and a new group of people came running into the compound and rushed into the house. Some had drums, on which they beat a frenzied tattoo. Their eyes were staring and bloodshot, and some of them were flecked with blood-stained spittle. They had been drinking the potent Palm-toddy and also smoking bhang and were in a state of drunken, drugged frenzy – mad with the lust for killing. Leonardo realised that they were Musungulos who had gone over to the Omanis.

They came out of the house, dragging with them Nunes' wife and child who had been hiding inside. They took no notice of the woman's screams for mercy, nor of the attempts of the original group of Omanis to rescue their prisoners, whom they wanted for slaves. Seizing the child, one of the men drew his panga and with one blow, severed his head from his body. His father could only groan and struggle to free himself from his bonds; the sweat poured down his face and his eyes stared from his head with the effort.

Then the woman tried to run to freedom, but they caught her and dragged her struggling and screaming back into the hut, from where her pitiful screams and moans, coupled with the laughs of the men, indicated to her demented husband that she was being raped. He fell into a coma, and it must have been some time later when he heard a noise and lifted his bloodshot eyes to see the men carrying his wife out of the hut to the edge of the bush, where they threw her lifeless body. They apparently thought he was dead, for apart from aiming a few kicks at him as they went past, they ignored him!

There was a silence and then Leonardo saw a flicker of flame break out from the roof of the hut – the devils had set it on fire! Soon it was blazing, and as the flames leapt, he could hear shouts and screams coming from other parts of the town.

Like a pack of hunting dogs on a new scent, the Musungulos left the hut to burn and ran off in the direction of the new commotion; still beating their drums as they went off in search of new mischief.

Nunes could see the still, lifeless body of his little son, lying in a pool of blood in the compound; the sight of the pathetic little figure lying so still made him burst into great wracking sobs. He calmed down a little, then all at once he heard a slithering noise coming towards him.

Cold sweat broke out all over him, for there were great pythons in the bushes and he was helplessly tied to the tree. However, when it came closer, he saw it was his wife, Fatima, who was still alive, although terribly injured; she was dragging herself painfully towards him.

She took a very long time to get to him, and she had to stop frequently to rest. Then, making a supreme effort, she reached up, using a knife she had found on the ground, laboriously cut through the ropes which bound his wrists and freed him. He quickly loosened the remaining ropes that held his ankles, and although very stiff, hobbled to her and took her in his arms; but the effort had been too much for her battered body and she started to vomit blood.

"Go! Go and avenge our son. I'm dying, but you must live to avenge him."

She passed into a coma and it was not long before she went limp and he felt a chill go through her. She had died saving him! Leonardo gently lowered her body to the ground. There was no time to bury the dead, for if he delayed he might be captured and her sacrifice would have been in vain. Weeping violently he had to leave the bodies of his beloved wife and son where they lay, and slink off to hide in the thick bush.

The next few hours passed like a nightmare. He was dazed with grief and found himself wandering through the bush to the water's edge. The tide was quite low and he wandered along the beach. He could see the glare of a great fire, and the sound of thumping drums seemed louder. He crept towards the fire carefully, taking great care to remain concealed and not reveal his presence by snapping twigs or crackling leaves. Reaching the edge of the bush, he took a cautious peep at the scene in front of him.

He could see a circle of figures and the sight made him gasp with horror, for they were the Musungulos from the mainland! They were smallish men and women, and as he crept nearer he could catch the strong, oily smell emanating from them as they danced around the fire. Their bodies glistened with sweat and oil, their eyeballs were glassy and staring as they undulated their bodies in time to the throbbing of the drums. Their faces were painted and their teeth blackened and filed to sharp points. Every now and then they would break into a loud, shrill trilling sound.

Suddenly the dancing changed in rhythm. The drumming quickened and the dancers whirled faster around the fire; heads, buttocks, shoulders and stomachs all gyrating in an ever-increasing tempo.

Before Leonardo's terrified eyes, a witch-doctor sprang into the centre of the circle and started whirling furiously around.

This strange figure wore a kilt of leopards' tails, and the head of the beast on his head like a cap. The paws, complete with its sharp claws, were like gloves on his hands. Strings of shark's teeth, cowrie shells and a couple of small skulls were strung around his neck; his costume was completed by shells and metal bells tied to his knees ankles. Leonardo crossed himself hastily, in spite of having changed his religion!

The witch-doctor danced around the fire in a maniacal frenzy and finally called out something in a shrill voice. The other dancers immediately took up the cry and Leonardo saw a terrified Swahili woman being dragged through the bushes by a couple of Musungulos, closely followed by two men in the centre of another howling horde of men. All three were thrown on the beach near where Leonardo was crouched in hiding.

Then the men were seized again and rushed up the beach to where the witch-doctor was waiting; leaving the woman tied up and lying on the sand. The witch-doctor ordered the men to be laid out on the sand, their arms and legs spread-eagled and tied to stakes buried in the sand. He then danced around them, the drums beating a furious tattoo; the people broke into a weird, high-pitched chant; and the flames leapt higher as more brushwood was piled on the fire.

The witch-doctor whirled around the prostrate men, brandishing a knife and then suddenly swooped. There was a long-drawn outcry of agony which stopped with a gurgle. The witch-doctor lifted his knife high in the air in triumph, then raised his other hand above his head. It held a bleeding object – he had cut off the man's head!

Again he swooped and there was another shriek, and once again the fiend lifted the severed head of his victim, and Leonardo could see that the knife and his arms were red in the firelight.

Leonardo saw the Musungulos were all intent on watching the witch-doctor, and that no watch was being kept on the woman who was lying on the beach with wide terror-stricken eyes. He crawled slowly on his stomach until he reached her side. "Make no noise!" he whispered into her ear. "I am a friend!" Swiftly cutting through her bonds, he motioned to her to follow him.

In spite of her stiffness, she silently crawled back with him to the shelter of the bushes, then as soon as they were a safe distance from the beach, they stood up and ran hand in hand away from the dreadful scene. When they at last halted to catch their breath, the woman told Leonardo that the men who had been butchered were her husband and his brother.

The next two days were spent making their way very cautiously towards the Fort; keeping to the bush and avoiding houses. They saw and heard the most dreadful things, but carried on their way, stopping only to quench their thirst with the juice of some coconuts they found stacked outside a deserted hut. Leonardo saw some mangoes hanging from a tree in the compound, and climbing up, was able to pick a few and dropped them down to the woman below.

They travelled only by night, and went very cautiously, hiding themselves in deep bush during the day. Eventually they saw the great walls of the Fort looming ahead of them and made their way to the gate. They shouted for help, until at last the gate swung open and they were admitted.

Leonardo Nunes was a broken man and had but one burning desire in his heart – revenge!

Chapter 26

One morning, early in November, Carlos got up before dawn and made his way into one of the watch-towers. He loved watching the sunrise and this was an ideal position from which to do so.

He looked towards the north as the sun rose out of the sea to the east, and there, quite close, he saw the sails of approaching ships. He shouted out a warning, then as they drew nearer, he could see it was the long-expected Portuguese fleet. Carlos shouted with joy and soon everyone in the Fort was preparing to welcome Commander Pereira da Silva back.

This time they landed without, any opposition from the Omani, but could only stay a few hours as they were on their way to Mozambique for Christmas. However, they left a few men and some stores (all da Silva had been able to persuade the Governor of Goa to give him) and, taking some of the very sick men on board, set sail again in the evening.

Before he left, Pereira da Silva promised to call at Mombasa on his way back to Goa, saying he would pick up some passengers. Maria and her mother were delighted, for they were to leave Mombasa with Joseph and Carlos.

There was a new air of expectancy and the talk was all of Goa. As the fleet would be away for several weeks, the women started making their preparations by bringing out the great carved camphor-wood chests which held their possessions. These chests had been stored away for many months, and now all their free time was spent in mending and renovating their clothes.

While the fleet had been unloading stores, the Fleet Comander came ashore for a couple of hours, bringing with him Captain Leandro Barbosa. He had arrived as second in command to Joseph de Britto, and would eventually take over the command of the Fort when Joseph returned to Goa with his family.

Joseph looked at his new officer and saw a heavy, middle-aged man, with a florid complexion, a thick neck, close-cropped iron grey hair, and a mouth like a rat trap – without pity or humour! He greeted Joseph civilly enough, but his small eyes were roving all over the Fort while da Silva and Joseph were talking.

When he joined in the conversation, he made no secret of the fact that he considered himself a strict disciplinarian, and Joseph gathered from what he said, that floggings and hangings were inevitable in the cause of 'good discipline' and obedience. Joseph thought wryly to himself that if this was the man's attitude, God help the defenders of the Fort. He would soon find himself without a command, for sickness carried off enough men, without the Commandant killing any!

A new priest, Father Rodrigues, had also arrived from Goa, and Joseph thought to himself that he would make a very suitable companion for the new Commandant!

This man was very different to their beloved Father Antonio. He was tall and thin, with a gaunt face and a sallow complexion caused by years of fasting and scourging. He was also completely bald. There was nothing soft or yielding about him. Compassion was foreign to his nature. He had come to save souls and had no room in his heart for pity or charity nor did he make any allowances for the human weaknesses of other people.

The God he believed in was the God of the Old Testament – an avenging God of wrath, not a God of love like Father Antonio's. He at once deplored the fact that there were Muslims in the Fort, and he referred to them as 'those heathens'. He burned with a fanatic zeal and his ambition was to introduce the methods of the Inquisition to this heathen land, starting with the inmates of the Fort!

He at once took an intense dislike to the gentle, learned Sheikh Abdulla, whom he saw as the Devil's right-hand man, and he succeeded in conveying this dislike to Leandro Barbosa, who was already casting his eyes around the Fort in search of someone he could bully. "With a man like this," Joseph thought, as he looked into the Priest's hard, black eyes, "there's no rejoicing at the birth of Christ, but he's the type who would get pleasure out of his Calvary!"

Joseph gave a little shudder and felt very glad he was leaving and would not have to serve with these men for many weeks. The events of the next few days really convinced him!

Leandro Barbosa showed his contempt for the Muslims by deliberately trying to treat the Prince of Faza's retinue as servants – an attitude they resented bitterly.

It all blew up to a head one evening, when Leandro Barbosa saw Sheikh Abdulla passing and, whispering to the Priest, who was standing next to him glowering at the old man, said, "Watch this! I'll make the old crow jump!"

He shouted to Abdulla to pick up a box which was lying nearby and carry it to his quarters. Sheikh Abdulla calmly ignored him and went on his way, while Leandro spluttering with rage, yelled after him, "You'll be sorry for that, you filthy old crow!"

Prince Daud, who was quietly watching, went pale, and his hand strayed to the curved dagger at his side at the deliberate insult to the old Sheikh. But he kept his temper, and striding over to Leandro Barbosa, deliberately stood in front of him and looked him up and down.

Then he stared into the man's eyes and said in an icy voice, "Sheikh Abdulla is our Priest, and neither you nor any other Christian will insult him. Nor will you insult any of my people, who are free Muslims!"

He turned on his heel and stalked off proudly before either Leandro Barbosa, or the Priest, who had been standing next to him with his mouth open in amazement, could say a word.

As soon as he left, however, Leandro Barbosa turned to the Priest and said in a vicious voice, "He will suffer for that, just you wait and see my friend!"

The Priest agreed. "It's intolerable for a heathen to be allowed to speak to a Christian like that!" he said, and the two men continued railing against the Muslims.

In the meantime Prince Daud had gone straight to Joseph and told him of Barbosa's insulting behaviour and the fact that the Priest had stood by and encouraged him.

"I will not tolerate insults, either to myself or to my people," he told Joseph passionately. "There will be blood spilt between us when you go, so to avoid this, I and my people will leave with you."

Joseph calmed him down, and after some discussion, it was decided that Prince Daud, Hussein, Sheikh Abdulla and a few old servants would go with him to Goa; the rest of his people would leave the Fort and make their way to Faza.

Joseph called for Leandro Barbosa to come to see him in his quarters, accompanied by the Priest. When the two men arrived, he gave them a severe warning about their behaviour.

"Prince Daud and his people are our friends and allies," he told them. "And if it had not been for their help, Fort Jesus would have been in Omani hands long ago! I want it very clearly understood by you two men that for as long as I am Commandant of this Fort, everyone – and I mean everyone, irrespective of colour or creed – will be treated with consideration and courtesy. I want no repetition of this disgraceful behaviour – especially from men who are supposed to set an example to the rest of the Fort!" Then he added in a very frigid tone, "You will be responsible to me for your future actions!"

Leandro Barbosa glared at him, but as Joseph was still his superior, he decided to keep quiet for the time being. After all, it was only a matter of weeks before Joseph was to leave.

"Then they will see who is master of this Fort!" he said to the Priest, as soon as they were out of Joseph's hearing. "Just let them wait until then."

There was comparative peace after this, for Prince Daud and his men took care to keep out of Leandro Barbosa's way and to avoid the Priest; but all the same, there was an unpleasant air of tension in the Fort, which had nothing to do with the Omani!

Chapter 27

Christmas came once more to the Fort, but this time it was a very different Christmas to the one they had celebrated so happily a year ago.

The women made an effort to decorate the Chapel, but the new Priest was very disapproving and their thoughts were sad ones, for they remembered their beloved Father Antonio and the joy he had brought to Christmas. Now he was dead, together with so many others; the only people left, out of the original defenders of the Fort, were Joseph and Maria, Hadija, Carlos, Prince Daud, Hussein, Sheikh Abdulla, Leonardo Nunes and a handful of Prince Daud's people!

The day passed quietly. The Christians all went to Mass at midnight, but as soon as it was over, they dispersed quietly to their own quarters. Joseph and Maria, however, walked for a little while on the ramparts and watched the bright stars shining above them. There was quiet joy in their hearts, for Maria was now expecting a child.

The night was warm and there was a soft breeze blowing. In the distance they could hear sounds of voices and singing. The breeze rustled the fronds of the palm trees below and the soft lapping sound of the waves at the foot of the Fort was carried to them. There was the shrill sound of the cicadas, and occasionally they could see a bat momentarily silhouetted against the starlit sky.

It was very calm and peaceful. Whatever blood had been shed in and around Fort Jesus, these moments would be there. It was a moment of peace and happiness for Joseph and Maria.

A few days later, the old year, with its sadness and sorrow came to an end, and they knelt once more in the Chapel praying for their future. When they came out, the year 1698 had already dawned.

Carlos and Hussein thought there should be something special happening to mark the beginning of the new year and, to their joy, as they crossed the courtyard from the Chapel, they looked up at the sky in time to see a sudden flash of silver as star fell to earth.

The boys were thrilled – they had had a visible sign from Heaven that the new year had begun! Of course Hussein, being a Muslim, had a different new year, but he had waited for Carlos outside the Chapel and they always celebrated all their holidays and feast days together. Carlos drew the line at fasting during Ramadhan, but joined in the celebration of Idd, which marked the end of the fast!

It was rare to see one of the boys without the other. This was a friendship which was to endure, and throughout their lives they were closer than brothers. They were eleven years old now, and had matured a lot during the past few months. They were growing tall and gangling and, like all adolescent boys, thought they had already reached manhood. Carlos' voice had begun to break, but to his annoyance, Hussein's voice retained its childish treble. Carlos was even sure he could see the beginnings of a beard, and spent a lot of time in front of a mirror, looking hopefully at his chin!

They were both much quieter now, for the horror of losing their loved ones had left its mark on them. Hussein mourned for his beloved brother, and Carlos deeply regretted the death of his father; they both missed their beloved friend and teacher, Father Antonio.

Although Carlos would never have admitted it, for he considered it an unmanly weakness, Maria knew that he sometimes cried himself to sleep at night. She said nothing to him in order to save his pride, but she went out of her way to show affection to the young orphan. He responded eagerly, and a very close bond grew up between them, which was to last a lifetime. Maria gradually took the place of his beloved mother and gave him the feminine love and attention he needed.

Hussein, on the other hand, turned to his cousin Prince Daud, and Sheikh Abdulla for comfort. His aunt, Hadija, was also always ready to listen to his troubles. In spite of their widening interests, the boys' affection for each other remained as strong as ever.

After New Year, Carlos felt sad, for he knew he would be leaving behind all he had known since he was a baby; he realised subconsciously that as soon as he left Mombasa for Goa he would be stepping across the threshold into manhood.

He had a sudden desire to be alone, and took to getting up very early in the morning and going along to a vantage point where he could watch the sun rise from behind the rim of the horizon like a golden ball. He would watch the sea and sky grow lighter, and see them suddenly glow with colour. As the sun rose, the green of the trees seemed more vivid, and he would catch his breath at the beauty of the soaring, wheeling, swooping birds. This was something he would remember and treasure all his life.

Gradually he stored up precious memories and conditioned himself for the break that had to come. As he did so, he thought of his parents and determined he would make a success of his life and become the kind of man they would have been proud to call their son!

Chapter 28

In the second week of January a new period of horror began. The doctor came running to Joseph one day, his face white with fear. It took him several minutes to calm himself enough to gasp out his news.

"The plague has broken out again, and already two men have died!"

"Oh God! Not again!" Joseph groaned and put his head in his hands. Then recovering himself, he snapped out, "Keep everyone away and burn the bodies!"

"I've done so already, but they've been in close contact with the others for weeks. They were amongst the reinforcements who arrived in December. It's their first time on overseas duty; they went straight to Goa from Portugal; then they had the long journey here. That must have weakened them, for they've no resistance to the disease. They fell ill and within a matter of hours they were dead. There's nothing I can do!"

The man swayed as he spoke and Joseph noticed with horror that his eyes were glazed as he fell to the floor.

"God preserve us!" he gasped, "you too are ill!" He went at once to see if he could find help. There were a few men left who had had the plague before and had recovered, so he called two of them to carry the doctor to the sick quarters.

Great fires were built and the clothing and possessions of all the sick men were burnt, but in spite of all these precautions, the plague raged through the Fort and men continued to sicken and die.

The doctor died very soon, closely followed by the Priest. Each new day brought several new cases, until after a few weeks scarcely any fit people remained to nurse and bury the dead. They were, of necessity, flung into a mass grave which had been dug outside the walls of the Fort, and although they were mourned, they were buried hastily and without any ceremony. Very few of those who fell ill with the plague survived.

Dysentery too, took its toll among the survivors, and by this time it was useless having a special place for the sick. They lay in sheltered corners all over the Fort. The heat had increased, bringing greater discomfort to everyone in the Fort. Maria, Hadija and a handful of other women worked valiantly amongst the sick and dying until they grew thin and weak with fatigue.

"You must rest!" Joseph said to them as he came upon them ministering to the sick one day. He noticed their pale faces, their hair hanging in lank strings, wet with perspiration, their damp dresses clinging clammily to them. But they carried on somehow, snatching a few hours restless sleep whenever they could. By now their medical supplies were finished and all they could do was to bring a little comfort to the sick and dying; sponging a burning hot body with cool water to give a moment's relief, smoothing a fevered brow. But in spite of their valiant efforts the disease took its deadly toll before it at last slackened off.

Hadija went wearily to Joseph, depressed and upset. "We must have some medicine to make a brew which will cure the dysentery," she told him. "We'll have to risk sending my slave, Ali, out of the Fort to gather herbs. He's small but clever, and I doubt whether the Omani would notice him!"

Joseph was reluctant, for he had noticed the Omani gathering in the heavy bush around the Fort, and suspected that if they realised how bad the situation was inside the Fort, they would not hesitate to attack, and with a good chance of success. However, after much pleading, Hadija persuaded Joseph to let Ali go. It was an ugly incident which brought about his reluctant agreement!

Even as Hadija was speaking to him, trouble had flared up between Leandro Barbosa and Prince Daud. This had come about because the Prince had suddenly come round the corner of one of the buildings in time to see and hear Leandro Barbosa shouting and attacking Sheikh Abdulla, who had been quietly kneeling on his praying mat facing Mecca. Prince Daud saw Barbosa take a kick at the kneeling man, and heard him shout, "Get up and away from there, you filthy heretic! It is you and the dirty scum like you that have brought this plague upon us!"

Barbosa was beside himself and foaming with rage. Still shouting curses, he fell on the poor old man like madman, kicking him in the ribs and stomach. The old man covered his white hair and tried to protect his head with shaking hands, as Barbosa tugged off his turban and aimed a vicious kick at him.

Prince Daud, his face pale with rage, drew his sword and ran to the rescue of the old Sheikh, whom he loved like a father. Leandro Barbosa saw him coming, and his sword was at once in his hand as he turned to meet his foe. Sparks flew as the two sharp pieces of steel clashed together.

"You filthy, cowardly son of a pig," snarled the Prince, "attacking a helpless old man. On guard and fight for your life, for I mean to kill you!"

The sound of the angry voices and the clash of swords brought Joseph and several other men running, but although Joseph shouted at them to stop fighting, the two antagonists were too angry to hear him and continued to slash at each other. Leandro Barbosa lunged at the Prince just as he slightly lowered his guard; his sword went through the Prince's right side, but fortunately not too deeply.

"Stop fighting! Stop it this instant!" shouted Joseph, and ordered Leonardo Nunes and the other men to hold the two assailants apart.

"Have we not enough troubles without the defenders of the Fort cutting each other down?" Joseph spoke bitterly. "What was the reason for this fight?"

Leandro Barbosa was foaming with rage, and his eyes were blootshot and staring. Three men had to hold on to him to prevent him from attacking the Prince again, so Joseph turned to Prince Daud.

"Look behind you," said the Prince angrily, "and you will see why I drew my sword!"

Joseph had only had eyes for the fighting men when he dashed on the scene, but now he turned to where the Prince pointed his accusing finger and saw a pathetic body huddled by the wall, motionless! He gasped as he saw it was Sheikh Abdulla – his white head bare and his beard streaked with blood from his injured mouth where Barbosa had kicked him. Rushing over, Joseph slipped his arm gently under the frail old man's head, but it was too late! The pain and shock had killed the old man and his eyes gazed sightlessly upwards.

Prince Daud came and stood next to Joseph, his face pale and drawn with sorrow and pain. He swayed as he told Joseph the story. "That dog is mad!" he concluded bitterly, and indeed, Leandro Barbosa had slipped over the edge of sanity!

For the time being Joseph ordered that he be shut up, a prisoner, in the Bastion of San Antonio. Prince Daud's people sadly took the battered body of their old Priest away for burial, and Joseph put his arm around the young Prince and took him to Hadija, who dressed his wound.

The cut soon became inflamed, and by that evening Prince Daud was tossing with pain and fever.

Hadija went to Joseph again in despair and said, "My son, I must have fresh herbs if my nephew's life is to be saved. There are the leaves of a certain bush which when boiled and applied as a poultice reduces the pain and swelling. We also need other herbs. You promised to let my slave Ali fetch them from outside the Fort. I beg you, let him go before it is too late!"

Joseph had to agree and that night they hung a strong basket on a rope, and quietly lowered the boy on the darkest side of the Fort. He gave the rope a tug when he reached the ground and at once slipped quietly away into the bushes. His home was outside the town and it was thought that he would be able to go through the Omani who were camped around the Fort.

Anxiously they waited throughout the next day, by which time Prince Daud was very ill and barely conscious. As soon as darkness had fallen, the basket was again lowered and to their relief they soon felt the rope tugged as a signal that Ali was ready to be hauled into the Fort again. His mission had been successful for he carried several big bunches of various herbs in a bag tied to his back. He said that he had been able to slip past the Omani easily.

Hadija soon had a fresh poultice on Prince Daud's wound and all that night they kept anxious watch over him. At last, as dawn came and lightened the sky, they knew that with careful nursing he would live.

The plague was now over, but only a few people remained out of the hundreds who had been in the Fort a few weeks before. Time was running out for them, and the survivors knew it would not be long before the Omani realised how weak the defences of the Fort were, and attacked again.

The fleet was due from Mozambique any day now, and the fate of the Fort was a race between the Omani attackers and the Portuguese ships.

Joseph took stock of his remaining forces, then sat motionless with despair, his head in his hands. The position was hopeless! Besides himself, Jacome de Morais, Leonardo Nunes and about fifteen Swahilis were the only fit men left! His other resources were Leandro Barbosa, who was now completely insane and had to be kept under lock and key, the two young boys, Hussein and Carlos, who were both brave but yet so young; Prince Daud, who was still a very sick man; Maria and her mother and three Swahili women. This was his total defence force! They were helpless, and Joseph knew that should the Omani attack the Fort again, they would all fall to the enemy.

After sitting and thinking quietly for a while, he decided that, although he intended defending the Fort to the last, the time had now come to make plans for the escape of the survivors. He called the other men to him and it was decided that Leonardo Nunes could easily pass for a Swahili having lived amongst them. Therefore he could slip quietly out of the Fort by the secret tunnel and contact his wife's people, who were fishermen on the other side of the island. He would arrange with them to sail a small dhow around the island by night, and hide it carefully amongst the mangrove swamps at the base of the coral cliffs below Fort Joseph. This dhow was to be provisioned with food and water.

Time was short, so that very night Leonardo slipped away through the tunnel, and after seeing that all was clear, he made his way through the darkness.

Those in the Fort were tense with fear during the three days that Leonardo was away; however, on the third night he returned quietly through the tunnel and told Joseph that the dhow had been hidden successfully and would remain there should they need it.

In the meantime, Joseph had had their few belongings carried down to the cave near Fort Joseph's in readiness for their possible escape.

Now it was a matter of waiting for the attack, which they all knew must come soon. They were all determined to fight to the death rather than fall into the hands of the enemy for they knew that capture would mean torture and enslavement.

Chapter 29

Two days later the expected assault on the Fort began. The enemy were cautious at first, for they were unsure of the strength of the defences, but they soon realised the weakness of the defenders and doubled their attacks.

Everyone, including the women and the young boys fought valiantly, but at last Joseph realised that it was only a matter of an hour or so before the Fort would be in the hands of the enemy. Now was the time for putting their plans of escape into action!

The first scaling ladders were actually scraping against the wall when Joseph gave the signal for them to go, and the small party left their defensive position and raced to the store.

As Joseph reached the door of the store he stopped in his tracks as he realised that Leandro Barbosa was still a prisoner in the Bastion. The man was mad, but he was one of their own people and Joseph felt he could not leave him to torture and death. Time was running out and now this delay could mean death to them all.

As Joseph hesitated and looked back towards the Bastion, Jacome read his thoughts and ran across to him saying urgently: "Hurry! You must take the women and the others to the dhow. They must be saved at all costs. Don't worry, Leonardo and I will fetch Leandro Barbosa and, after blowing up the store-room, we'll follow you to the dhow. Don't wait for us. If we haven't come by midnight, then leave without us, for you'll know something has gone wrong. Go now, and make haste!"

The men shook hands and parted.

"May God be with you," Joseph said as he turned away. "Follow us as soon as you can!"

He entered the store-room and made his way to the end of the passage and onwards to the cave where the rest of the party were waiting for him. Prince Daud was still very weak, and had been helped down the passage by a couple of his men. Maria and Hadija stood near him and were guarded by four other men who had also managed to escape. Hadija had allowed her small slave Ali to leave them and go to his home; he had been lowered from the Fort in a basket for the last time earlier that evening. Both Carlos and Hussein carried their swords in their hands and although so young, were prepared to fight to the death if necessary. There were also two Swahili women who had escaped with them. The rest of the men had been killed whilst fighting off the first attack on the Fort.

Joseph gathered together his little band of refugees, and hurried them out into the darkness. He knew his way well, and they followed him closely as he crept silently through the bush and took the path which led down the coral cliff to where the dhow had been hidden. Two of the men half-carried Prince Daud, and the other four carried their few precious possessions.

As noiselessly as they could, they made their way until at last Joseph whispered to them to halt. He searched along the edge of the water and at last found the canoe. It had been carefully hidden amongst the rocks and covered with bushes. He soon uncovered it and, helped by one of the men, pushed it into deeper water.

One by one he ferried his little party and their loads to the dhow which was anchored in deeper water, yet hidden from the shore by mangroves. At last they were all safely on board. Then, as it was late, they settled down to an anxious wait. The moon rose and shone peacefully down on them.

Half an hour had passed, and they were all silent and tense, listening for the slightest sound as they strained their eyes into the shadows cast by the moonlight, alert for the slightest movement.

"What was that?" A dull 'BOOM' had achoed through the night from the direction of the Fort, and there was a sudden red glow in the sky. Maria gave a start of fright and clung to Joseph's arm.

"That must have been Jacome and Leonardo blowing up the store-room!" Joseph whispered. "They should be here soon!"

Again the party on the dhow settled down to wait uneasily and Joseph paddled the canoe back to the shore. The time seemed to drag and he could hear his own breathing, which seemed very loud in the deep silence of the night.

At last he heard a slithering sound coming down the path and called softly, "Who is it?"

"Jacome!" came the panted reply, only just audible. "Leonardo is dead and I'm wounded. You'll have to help me. I've lost a lot of blood and I'm very weak."

Joseph scrambled up the path and found his friend. In the moonlight he could see he was spattered with blood from several wounds. He put his arm around him and helped him carefully to the canoe. As they reached the side of the dhow, willing hands reached down and the two men were helped aboard.

"Make haste! We must go at once!" Jacome said urgently. "The Omani will be like disturbed ants swarming all over the island soon, and it will go very ill with us if we're caught now. We must get away from here with all speed!"

The sail on the little craft was raised and they soon managed to bring it into the wind, and in a few moments they were moving out of the harbour southwards. It was none too soon! As they began to move away from the shore, they heard shouts coming towards them from the Fort; but the Omani were too late to capture them, and they were out of range by the time the enemy reached the beach and fired in their direction. They had escaped with a very narrow margin of safety!

Soon the breeze became stronger and they were out of sight of the harbour and heading swiftly south.

Chapter 30

When at last they were safely on their way, Jacome told them the story of his escape:

"Just as Leonardo and I reached the Bastion of San Antonio, the Omani launched another attack on the Fort. We managed to get inside and free Leandro Barbosa, but he refused to come with us, saying he preferred to die where he was. The man was quite mad! Leonardo and I looked at each other and then turned to leave him, for we could not drag him away by force and we had already risked our own lives by returning to rescue him.

"By this time we had left it rather late and the Omani were already swarming over the walls and running towards us.

"'Get back to the store-room before it's too late,' shouted Leonardo to me. 'Run as fast as you can!'

"We started running but were intercepted by the first Omani. Desperately we struggled with them, and because we knew we were fighting for our lives, we fought with the fury and strength of a dozen men. We soon managed to fight our way clear and ran towards the store-house. We swung the heavy door back in the faces of the enemy who were following close on our heels. We struggled frantically until the strong metal bar at last slipped into place. We had a few moments respite while the men outside shouted, and then after some consultation, they went off, presumably in search of something with which to batter down the heavy door. We were both wounded, but Leonardo's wounds were worse than mine.

"As he lay against a wall, coughing, I crawled up to the door again and put my eye to a slit. It was bright moonlight outside, and I found I could see the courtyard of the Fort quite clearly, and the entrance to the Bastion of San Antonio. Just as I looked towards it, I saw Leandro come rushing from the door, his sword flashing in his hand. He was immediately pounced on by the Omani. He fought bravely, but in no time he was hacked to pieces by the scimitars of the Omani.

"Our wounds were bleeding freely and Leonardo had received a sword-thrust which had pierced his lung. He began to cough blood. After a bout of coughing, he turned and said to me:

"'I'm dying, my friend, but before I die I wish to take as many of these dogs with me as possible to avenge my wife and son! You must go now and join the others – this is my wish. There's no need for us both to die!'

"I protested, but Leonardo grew angry with me.

"'You must go,' he insisted. 'But before you go we must make sure the tunnel is blocked at this end. I need your help for a moment, then you must go so that I can carry out my plan. Help me to roll some of those barrels to the entrance of the tunnel!'

"I did as he asked, and very soon we had piled several barrels against the entrance of the tunnel. Leonardo then laid down a trail of gunpowder to the barrels and said to me with a grim smile:

"'Go now, Jacome, for my time is getting short and I want you well out of the way when our enemies force their way in here. Before you leave, help me onto that heap of barrels over in the corner. That's it! Now lay another trail of gunpowder from here to the entrance of the tunnel. These barrels all contain gunpowder, and it's my plan to let them batter down the door – in fact, as you hear, they've already started! As they swarm in, I'll light the trail of gunpowder with the taper I have ready here, and I hope to take as many of these dogs as possible with me! Now, don't protest, but just go, and may God go with you, my friend!'

"With tears in my eyes I complied with his wishes and, after helping him to take up his chosen position in a corner of the room, facing the door, I shook him by the hand.

"'Farewell, brave friend!' I said. He gave me a crooked smile and raised his hand as I turned away.

"I gave a last glance behind me before I entered the passage, and I saw the wood of the door beginning to splinter with the force of the heavy blows rained on it from the outside. I wasted no more time, but made my way as swiftly as I could, in spite of my wounds, down the passage, and soon I was a good distance from the store-room.

"All at once it seemed as though the whole ground had heaved itself up under me. I was thrown to the ground as a great BOOM resounded from the direction of the store-room. I could hear the sound of falling rocks behind me and then I became quite deaf and dazed. Leonardo Nunes had carried out his plan!

"After a few moments I recovered sufficiently to realise I must make my way as quickly as possible to where you were waiting for me."

Jacome fell silent for a moment, then he added very softly ... "He was a very brave man!"

Chapter 31

The little dhow sailed on southwards through the remainder of the night and soon after dawn the wind dropped and they carried on at a much slower pace.

It was nearly noon when Carlos, who had been appointed look-out, suddenly cried out, "Sails to the south!"

The men had been dozing on the deck, but soon roused themselves and looked in the direction of his pointing finger. They could see five big ships in the distance. They watched them approaching with some apprehension, but as they drew nearer, Joseph said: "We're saved by the Grace of God; for those are Portuguese ships ahead of us! It must be da Silva on his way to Mombasa to call for us – we must try and warn him!"

There was a flurry of activity as they set off on an intercepting course. Soon the leading ship came gracefully towards them and they all shouted and waved, until at last the lookout on the great ship saw them. Orders were shouted, and the ship changed course and came up to them, dropping sails as it did so. Faces looked down at them from the high side of the ship and a rope was thrown down. Then sailors dropped down into the dhow and helped them aboard the ship.

"Thank God we're now safe!" whispered Maria as Joseph took her hand gently and lead her forward. Their old friend Commander Pereira da Silva hurried up to greet them. It had been a great ordeal for her, and seeing how pale she was, the Commander wasted no time in seeing them to the cabins which had already been prepared.

"I was looking forward to having you on board my ship," he said, "but under happier circumstances than these. Anyway, we're still some way from Mombasa, so rest a while, and your husband and Captain de Morais will tell me the story." Joseph saw Maria and her mother calmly settled, and then made his way to the Commander's cabin to make his report.

Dusk had fallen by the time they had finished their discussions. Joseph called Maria up onto the deck and they stood together as the darkness fell. The sea rushed past the wooden sides of the ship with a soft sound, and the sails and masts creaked as the wind drove them onwards through the water. The moon came up at last, only to disappear behind a bank of clouds.

"We'll be off Mombasa harbour in less than an hour," Joseph said. "The Commander has told me that our force is not strong enough to launch a counter-attack, for the Fort will be strongly defended, but he will go in as close as he dare and the fleet will bombard the Fort from the mouth of the harbour. It won't achieve anything, but it will at least show the Omanis that we still have teeth, and that one day we will return and re-take Fort Jesus!"

Soon the moon broke out from behind the clouds, and as it did so, the people on board the ships could see the massive shape of the Fort looming up against the land. They had managed to sail quite close without being seen!

There was a sudden scurrying around and shouting of orders, then with a great "Boom!" the guns started firing at the Fort. They bombarded it for almost an hour, and although the guns of the Fort answered back, their fire was neither accurate nor effective. At last the signal was given for the guns to cease fire.

Joseph, Maria and the other survivors had stood together during the bombardment, quite dazed and deafened by the noise and confusion. Peace descended once more, and the ships turned about, facing north, and were brought into the wind. The smoke of the bombardment blew away and in the moonlight they could see Fort Jesus silhouetted behind them for the last time.

The survivors gazed back at the Fort which had given them refuge and happiness, as well as danger and sorrow, and tears filled their eyes as they saw it standing there – proud, awe-inspiring and timeless.

The wind filled the sails, the sea rushed past the bows of the swiftly moving ships. They were on their way to Goa and a new life.

The little group stood together on the deck, straining their eyes until the great shape of the Fort finally blended with the darkness behind them. Then, with a sigh, they turned away.

The great siege of Fort Jesus had ended; a great many had died and only a few survived to remember it; but the Fort, after changing hands several times over the intervening centuries, still stands today – worn and aged, but towering and formidable.

www.ingramcontent.com/pod-product-compliance
Lightning Source LLC
LaVergne TN
LVHW092049060526
838201LV00047B/1310